Retrospective

AN EXISTENTIALIST LOVE STORY FROM BEIRUT 1982

Simone Paturel

ISBN: 1979888892
ISBN 13: 9781979888899

To my two sons, Alexandre and Leonard, that I love beyond the world

Saturday, September 16, 2017, marked the thirty-fifth anniversary of the Sabra and Shatila massacre, when hundreds of members of the Phalange party (a Lebanese Christian militia), under the approving eye of Israeli Defense Minister Ariel Sharon, entered Sabra and Shatila refugee camps in Beirut.

Over three thousand Palestinian refugees were killed. Among the victims were infants, children, pregnant women, and the elderly.

In December 1982, the UN General Assembly declared the massacre to be an act of genocide. Minister Ariel Sharon was forced to resign after a special Israeli investigative-panel inquiry declared him to be "personally responsible" for "ignoring the danger of bloodshed and revenge" and "not taking appropriate measures to prevent bloodshed."

Despite this, Ariel Sharon survived politically and became the prime minister of Israel from 2001 to 2006. Not a single responsible party for the massacre has ever been successfully convicted under the law.

The massacre at Sabra and Shatila is another tragic and horrifying chapter in Palestinian history. The bloody civil war in Lebanon and the subsequent Israeli occupation continues to haunt the surviving families affected by the violence.

https://fundraise.interpal.org/2

Prelude

THE DRIVER INSISTED on keeping to thirty miles an hour even on good roads, and while going through the villages, the vehicle frequently ground almost to a halt, forced as it was to negotiate trucks, motorcycles, bicycles, people, and cattle. The speed bumps added to the stop-start nature of their progress, and even the smaller villages seemed to have at least half a dozen of them. The journey wore on through the afternoon, the drone of the engine and heat of the 4×4 adding a soporific effect. Laura tried to sleep, only to be woken by potholes and the driver's periodic and half-mumbled attempts at conversation. She ignored the frequent suggestions to stop at all manner of 'craft' shops, where no doubt the driver would be well compensated, and her journey rumbled on.

The landscape changed from verdant to dry desert and back again within the span of a few hours. Rolling hills with cornfields and pastures were slowly replaced first by scrubland and then dusty, parched fields. The landscape was pitted with water holes—many of them dried up, probably drained by the cattle and goats driven across the country in search of water, raising large clouds of dust wherever they went. The dust met and mingled with small sandstorms as they lazily danced their way across the land.

The road rose again as they approached the hotel, and with it came rivers and a greening of the terrain. The taxi dropped her in the alley next to the hotel. The driver, an old man with round glasses and yellow teeth, opened the boot and handed her the small suitcase. The light rain had clouded his glasses, and as his hand reached out for a tip, she suddenly changed her mind and kept her change in case she wanted to buy a drink. He looked at her perplexed, then got into his taxi, slammed the door, and drove off. Alone in front of a heavy black metal gate, she grabbed her luggage and walked through to the small footpath.

She rang the bell and stood at the gate, waiting impatiently for someone to answer. A handsome young man appeared and opened the wrought-iron gate. His green eyes looked questioning, wondering what she was doing here alone in this remote place. She recognized something tender and unusual in his look; then he smiled at her. He asked whether she was Laura. She nodded, pleased at his friendliness. He seized her luggage and stood back to let her go down to the entrance. Walking in front of him, she felt the compelling need to turn round, and when she did he swiftly turned his head away.

Going down the pathway in the red-lemon light of a fading afternoon, she felt a sudden impulse to run away; the constraints of this small walk, where time seemed to stretch to ages, weighed on her, and she began to feel tired.

As they walked she noticed on the right elegant rows of vines leading to a very beautiful garden, an inviting place to sit and drink around a small but elegant swimming pool while dreaming of a better life—at least that is what she thought; she reckoned most people had less dramatic lives than her. After all not everyone was running after shadows of an unfulfilled life. On her left a white horse was tied up, and as she passed by, the bellboy warned her it might bite her if she came too close, as the previous owner had treated it badly.

At the end of the path was a 1950s' house, a modernist masterpiece meticulously preserved on the outside. The bellboy walked in front of her and held the door open for her. They walked into an entrance hall paved with sand-coloured triangular tiles. The interior was light and modern with a pale wide wooden stairway leading to an upper floor. She imagined upstairs rooms off a spacious light-filled landing with a high white stucco ceiling. As she turned her head to the right, Laura saw a cabinet displaying bottles of wine labelled *Las Montes*, the name of the house. She remembered Elias telling her the house produced its own wine.

While sitting in front of an empty desk waiting for the receptionist to appear, she thought about the ill-treated horse and imagined all the scenes with its previous owner. She wondered why someone would be cruel to a creature that couldn't speak—why the person would show a pathological sadism by exerting power over an animal—rather than taking it as a companion. She could understand an aggressive response to a threat or to overcome a sense of helplessness, but not this. Maybe he had been depressed or lonely in his pain that he wanted to share it somehow, and beating the horse was a kind of a self-punishment. Somehow his cruelty was a kind of surrender, she thought, the kind that makes you destroy what's left after a war has wrought its own destruction. It was a feeling she knew well, and in a way she admired the courage of someone who was able to show his feelings of failure. It was something she couldn't do; she was the coward, frustrated, her emotions leading to a discontent and anger that she kept for herself, hiding behind a smile when she was about to lose everything and particularly herself. She felt she was on the edge of disaster, and the sense of deprivation that had been with her since childhood made the world seem unpredictable and unsafe. She was caught up between two wars—the Lebanese civil war that raged outside and a war between her parents inside her house. The sense of loss it had shaped meant that later losses would make her react with greater severity. For the moment, however, nothing seemed to cause any aggravation apart from this obsessive love that she felt towards her childhood friend Elias.

A sudden breeze coming through a large open window startled her. The door behind the desk opened, and a blond girl came in. The girl introduced herself as Audrey, greeted Laura with an English accent, and asked for her passport so she could photocopy it.

Laura gave it to her, her hand shaking and hesitant, and in a trembling voice, she asked, "Sorry but why do you need the passport? My boyfriend booked the room under his name, and we are only staying until tomorrow."

Audrey answered very politely, "I'm not aware of another name on the booking list; all I have in the records is that a room was booked under the name of Laura Malak."

"Laura Bauvier," Laura corrected her abruptly.

"I see; maybe it's your maiden name? I'm sorry about that, but I still need your passport and please your credit card too. Can you sign at the bottom of this paper please? Don't worry; I will add the date of today, which is the ninth of August, 1997."

Laura turned red. "Why the credit card? I'm confused—surely the room must have been paid for at the time of the booking!"

"The room hasn't been paid for; I'm sorry about the confusion. Yes, normally we would ask for a credit card to be given at the time of the booking, but the gentleman who called said that you will be dealing with it."

"I see. Anything else? she asked nervously. Then she added, "Who is the owner of this hotel?"

"Oh yes. I almost forgot, but the gentleman left us a message that he sent you a package. I am still waiting for the post to arrive. As soon as I receive it, I will inform you. As for the owner, she is Mrs. Gibbs—Sally Gibbs."

More blood rushed to her face. Laura started to feel unwell. A thousand thoughts raced through her head and shot through her veins, it was a long day. It was already late. She just grabbed her credit card and gave it to Audrey. She picked up her phone, but it didn't work; there was no signal. Elias's absence was a physical reality and should be looked at objectively, she thought, but still she refused to accept it. She feared the uncertainty of his absence almost as much as she dreaded his ambiguous presence.

Elias was her childhood friend—tall and thin, with deep dark eyes beneath beautiful long eyelashes giving him a very profound and mystical look. There was something deeply sad and touching in his look that was profoundly nostalgic but of times that never existed. They met when they were ten years old, playing in the garage of the building where Laura lived. Elias was the best friend of her neighbour, Mounir, and they were an inseparable trio until she became a teenager. Later he became distant towards her. When she recalled their childhood, she sometimes wondered how long it had really lasted.

Laura noticed her hands were trembling as she gripped the chair; she knew then he would not come. She looked down at her ill-fitting skirt and dusty, cheap white shirt, and almost instantly tears ran down her face. She felt unwell with knots in her stomach; what a fool she was. Her mind went out of control; she couldn't understand herself and what it was that brought her here.

For the last year, her relationship with Elias was a strange, cold one, with few words. Behind these moments there were some insights, and yet it was so difficult for her to understand him.

"You become real when someone loves you," he had said to her one day.

"But when they actually tell you the word or with their actions?" she asked.

He gazed at her and then said, "If you believe by saying a word, you can do a good deed then by omitting to say it you have sinned. But love is not a sin or a good deed; love is love. Words are not these physical shapes that fill gaps in our lives. When you love someone, you should say it and do it and make it."

He looked away from her then and almost seemed bored. She realized that she had taken him out of his comfort zone. She had gone too far, and he probably wasn't prepared to give her what she expected from him. His silence was as heavy as his words. "I can't get through to you. I can't get through to you," she thought, but her words died on her lips. Laura hated him for his arrogance; he was so sure of himself.

Audrey brought back her credit card on a small silver plate with a pen to sign it. For one moment she thought she was being offered a drink; then, disappointed, she signed the receipt nervously.

The bellboy appeared and showed Laura to her room. The room was spacious, painted in white with a large wooden sleigh bed in the middle. The bed was flanked with two small bedside tables, and on each one of them was a gilded bronze lamp with crystal prisms. The wall on the left was hung with old family photographs and a portrait of a man with the name James Thompson written at the bottom. She thought his unsmiling expression indicated that he was from the upper class—only drunk, poor, innocent people smiled in those days. Next to the photograph, a torn piece of newspaper was framed. It read, "In a letter to the *Sacramento Daily Union*, Mark Twain wrote, 'A photograph is a most important document, and there is nothing more damning to go down to posterity than a silly, foolish smile caught and fixed forever.'" An explanation perhaps why this man didn't smile.

An oval mirror hung on the wall opposite the bed and next to it a large original wooden window frame. Looking through the window, she saw the white horse tied up. She looked at him and thought how similar she was to him, tied to a destiny she couldn't change. A sun beam shone on her face, and she saw millions of particles. And she tried to grasp some. For a moment she felt happy, but doubt over the room's price stayed in the back of her mind. Closing the door behind left her in a world of silence; only the sunbeam was her companion. She wished these particles could carry her to another world far from this one, with no thoughts. She was tired of her thoughts coming back to hit her as if she was constantly bouncing them back as a ball in a tennis court or as if waves were submerging her constantly with doubts.

Laura hated mirrors as they made her feel exposed; they showed the truth. Without them things would be different. Eyes are the equivalent of mirrors, she thought. Once Elias asked her why she loved so much to wear sunglasses although they didn't suit her. She pretended it was because she didn't want to get wrinkles, but actually she was very shy of showing her face. She didn't think of herself as beautiful. She tried to remove the mirror in front of her bed, but she couldn't lift it, as it was too heavy. She left it there and just sat on the edge of her bed, exhausted and slumped, like someone who'd just run a marathon. Life had suddenly weighed her down; she felt like a scapegoat in the desert, carrying the world's sins. But she had to play her part to gain salvation, a sort of old curse that she had to rid herself of. Her instant happiness flew with the sunbeams, dissolved itself in an ocean of her thoughts and worries. The mirror was there, like a judge. Seeing her stark reality of her troubled life bounced back at her. Her face was similar to her life stripped from any makeup—just plain.

Chapter I

SALLY WENT DOWN the round stairs, heading for reception, shaking off a long sleepy night when she saw the silhouette of Laura crossing the hall to the breakfast room. Her face lightened up, and she went to the registry book to see who had arrived last night. Scrolling down the names, she seemed to be looking for a missing one. Audrey rushed over to tell her about Laura and began gossiping about her. Sally interrupted and asked for a black coffee to be delivered as usual to her office and then went to chat with her guests in the dining room and proposed activities like horse riding or hunting or maybe a long walk. Guests often liked to stride off into the hills in search of nature.

The dining room was rectangular and elegantly decorated in a hunting-lodge style; the warm tones of wood and leather blended with gold and purple fabrics to create a very comfortable ambiance. A huge stag's head dominated the room above an old rectangular mirror with gold moulding, which sat over the black-marble fireplace. Daylight flooded in through six tall windows onto the slate floor, and at night the room was lit by a huge chandelier hung from the centre of the ceiling. She watched her guests; some of whom were still eating their breakfast while others were beginning to get up and leave. She approached Laura's table and with a warm smile asked her whether she had had a relaxing night. Clearly Laura was not in the mood to please and compliment the owner about the hotel and replied coldly that yes, it was OK. Sally pretended not to understand the tone and asked her if she wanted to join her later for a walk in the garden so she could show her the different plants and tell her their origin and also talk to her about the family history. Laura refused politely, pretending that she had a slight headache and preferred to be alone.

Sally excused herself, saying, "If you need any help, please tell me. I'll be very happy to show you around." She went back to her office, thinking about Laura, and then shook her head ruefully as she lifted her coffee to her lips, remembering her past.

Sally Gibbs was born in Kenya in 1948 to English parents escaping the continuing postwar austerity in Britain. Kenya had seemed to them an escape at the time, a sun-filled paradise far from the dreary and often smog-bound London. By the early 1960s, however, with Kenyan independence beckoning, the twelve-year old Sally went with her parents, Sarah and James Thompson, on a new adventure to South America. After six months in Buenos Aires, the family moved to Las Montes in Brazil, the small town where she would spend most of her life.

Sally had a strained relationship with her father from an early age. James Thompson was a severe character with black moods that sometime lasted for weeks on end.

Once in Las Montes, little changed. Thompson owned the village, and regular beatings ensued. Sally hated her father for the abuse he gave out to the farmers and longed to leave Las Montes.

At nineteen an offer for a place at Girton College in Cambridge proved irresistible, and Sally left Las Montes for what she hoped might be the last time. By the summer of 1968, she had met John Gibbs, a man with a gentle, laid-back nature. Despite the culture of free love that pervaded youthful society in the sixties, she married him in 1969 and was pregnant by 1970. Sally abandoned her studies and looked forward to a normal family life in contrast to her childhood. Her baby, Irene Gibbs, was born in April 1971.

John proved unsuccessful in life, with little ambition. By March 1972 the relationship had broken down. John had no job and no prospect of getting another. April 1972, however, brought news from Las Montes. A letter arrived from Sarah, the first communication since the birth of Irene. James was dead, killed in a cattle accident two weeks previously. There were no further details. Sally left England with Irene for Las Montes and never saw her husband again.

Sally Gibbs took control of her father's ranch. She was civil to the local population and popular but fared poorly as a farmer and ranch owner. As money grew tight, she had to gradually sell the land and cattle. Her mother died suddenly from a heart attack, and then six months later, her daughter Irene fell ill with influenza. After a fever lasting a week, and the local doctor still insisting she was suffering only from a common cold, Irene died. Sally buried Irene next to her mother in the garden of the house. She sold the remaining land except for that surrounding the house her father had built and opened her hotel.

She liked to take long strolls in the gardens or ride her horse for miles through neighbouring plains and forests. Riding was her favourite activity whenever she felt like running away from her life, from the memory of Irene. She had lost all faith in God by now and was adamant that God did not interfere in people's lives. For her God was an alien entity. "If you employ an architect to construct your house, you can't call him every time you have a problem," she often said to those who questioned her on religion. She felt that even with her life as it was, things would improve in one way or another. She was desperate to find love—a decent hardworking partner; all she wanted was to share her life with someone. Her distant cousin occasionally sent nice, wealthy men as hotel guests in the hope she would bond with one of them, but they were always eager to go back to the city and escape from such an isolated hacienda. It takes a lot to move here, she thought, and to be far from the chaos of city life, and not every man wants to hear his soul. The impermanence of things is more apparent in nature with the changing of seasons, death, and re-birth linked to the colour of the landscape, she thought. From white to pink to green to red to yellow, she saw them every year. It was like living in a spiritual eyrie, watching the secret of life unfold itself.

Her once-pale skin aged badly with too much sun first in Africa and then South America, but she was still a tall and very elegant woman.

A knock on the door brought her back to reality. The cleaning lady appeared through the door, but Sally dismissed her with her hand—"Come later, not now."

Once the door closed, she felt her hands shaking when thinking of Elias. Deep down she wished he would not turn up and that everything would return to the normal tedium as before. She picked up the phone and dialled his number as she implored God that she just wanted to hear his voice again. Then she put the phone down and Almost dropped to her knees knocking an ashtray to the floor. She placed her hand on the armchair to regain her balance, squeezing hard. She wished she had spoken to him for longer, days ago when he asked her to book the room for Laura.

Audrey interrupted her, "Are you OK? I just heard a noise." Sally shook her head dumbly, lost in her thoughts. Why? Why here? Why now? She did not think Laura recognized her or even knew who she was. She tried to stifle a cry of despair; she suspected Elias loved Laura. Her face contorted as a spasm of pain ripped through her; she was, for one stupid unthinkable moment, jealous. She hadn't seen Elias for almost a year, and she even wondered what he looked like now. Suddenly she opened her mouth in a moan of despair; she was longing for him.

->|=0 0=|<-

Laura switched in her mind from physical stress to emotional stress. She tried to understand why Elias's absence caused her such anguish. What astonished her was a world where all this was acceptable. She sat propped up by cushions, her mind drifting to the beginning of their story. With a grimacing smile as if some fluid was caught in her throat, she tried to remember the events that led her to meet Elias.

Hers was a highly educated bourgeois family touched by tragedy. Her mother lost her first child, a baby girl, in a car accident before Laura and her brother were born. Her father, Joseph, was Lebanese, born in Alexandria; he was a tough character, who became embroiled in Egyptian politics, opposing the Nasser regime. After several political arrests and a few jail terms, Joseph made his way to Lebanon. With his studies in law and languages—he spoke six—he became a lawyer and met his future wife. Asma, Laura's mother, came from a prestigious Palestinian family. After the Israeli-Arab war in 1948, Israel took control of 60 percent of Palestinian territory, triggering huge demographical change, forcing some seven hundred thousand Palestinians into exile. Her grandfather gathered the family together and moved them to Lebanon. Asma was engaged to an English diplomat in the British Embassy until she met and fell in love with Joseph and left her British fiancé. Life was not easy, and it was difficult to relinquish old privileges and to assume her new life with its burdens of war.

She blamed world leaders for the situation; she believed there was a conspiracy to annihilate the Christians in the Middle East. She would speak publicly about this 'big plan' and thought she could expose the injustice and consequences of it. The injustice she felt led to excessive aggression towards others. She thought of herself as a foreigner in her own land, being dehumanized. Violence was everywhere—violence against the past and the present. The legendary city of Beirut, the Venice of the Middle East, became displaced in people's imagination, in laments for the past and illusions for the future. In 1975 Lebanon was ravaged by a civil war that broke up after a series of killings of Maronites and Palestinians in East Beirut, in Ain El Roumana. That led to an attack on a bus, killing twenty-eight Palestinians. Later the war took another direction. It became a conflict where Syria and Israel got involved. Moreover many Muslims and Christians became divided internally. Beirut became a ghost town, divided between two parts, east and west, or the Christian side and the Muslim side. Its Ottoman architecture lying on the threshold of decay and destruction was a constant reminder to Laura's mother of the loss of a glorious past.

Her father, on the other hand, was offered the leadership of the *Kataeb* party, a right-wing Christian militia. He declined the offer as he disputed their notion of political engagement and their dishonesty and carelessness in sticking to the cause. He felt you could be patriotic without exploring the ways and means of political power. Her father retreated into silence, and her mother attacked him for being too silent. Reconciliation between them was forever difficult to achieve because of how they perceived the war. Her father loved Lebanon and could not speak ill of it; he did not want to leave and live abroad. Despite the everyday harshness, the aggression against the innocent, the threatening divisions between civilians and the failure of the military to put an end to war, he always thought that compromise and peace could be achieved. His ultimate journey after Egypt was to Lebanon. He had his own peculiar ways of forgetting the war; he sometimes wilfully experienced amnesia in disturbing attempts to avoid reality and often retreated into a kind of eternal optimism.

With growing dissatisfaction in their marriage, her father became helpless to curb his wife's discontent and sought refuge in drinking, womanizing, and gambling for long hours outside the house. Her mother was left at home with

Laura and her brother. He jeopardized all the family's wealth on the poker table and lost. There was never any attempt at an explanation as to why he did that. It became clearer that they were both very different and were drifting apart.

Laura was in despair seeing just to what point her father criticized her, and yet he continued with his discourse of the importance of Christian beliefs in justice, truth, love, and compassion. She confessed that these beliefs frequently put her at odds with her father's behaviour. She was angry with him sometimes and felt like telling him to stop the injustices he committed against her mother. But she was careful not to argue with him, as he had a spirit of vengeance, which prevented reconciliation. War went on inside and outside her home, and Laura continuously struggled to understand human relationships. Trying and failing to achieve reconciliation within her family, she felt that independence should be her first step towards self-determination. She began to think for herself, to have an independent mind, and often found herself in mental confusion. She found it hard to understand that laws, customs, and regulations that were often forgotten, were what held a society together.

Walid, Laura's brother, was engaged in politics, and nothing else mattered to him. He was obsessed with weapons and armaments and loved cutting out articles from newspapers and magazines about the latest tanks and military-aircraft technology. He was tall and heavy-set with nut-brown hair and beautiful lips. He was nervous and argumentative and liked to play the big brother and was extremely jealous of Laura's closeness to her father.

She was never close to her brother; they both slept in the same room but had two different lives. She barely spoke to him, and they never shared any friends. She wasn't allowed to speak to his girlfriends when they came home although a few of them would say hello to her. She always felt it unfair that boys were allowed to mix with girls but not the other way round. Her father was very adamant about her keeping the honour of the family intact. The less her father cared about Walid's reputation, the more he became obsessed with her behaviour.

As the war's violence increased by 1982, her father's dream of a truce became unachievable and hopelessly idealistic. The cruel logic of violence had rendered peace impossible. Both her parents sought refuge from their lost past, trying to escape the inevitable only to find themselves trapped in a constant decay, reminding them every day of their own mortality. They were resigned to using violence to stop violence. More and more Laura came to define herself through her difference from the rest of her family. She felt very vulnerable and lacked the maturity to work out the relationship between her and the world around her. She felt condemned to an eternal unchangeable present and left out of her dreams; then she sought refuge in them the moment she met Elias.

Laura struggled to find an identity; hers was fluid. Was she Lebanese? Her past was a recollection of collective histories from Alexandria to Palestine, and both of her parents had lost their roots. How could she understand nationalism if her sense of history was lost? Only shared experience could identify her with Elias and his friends.

As she turned thirteen, Laura only exchanged looks and a few words with Elias. Sometimes when they met on the stairs, she felt he stripped her naked with his piercing eyes, and this made her feel uncomfortable. She didn't think of herself as a beautiful girl with her frizzy hair. He was always polite and courteous towards her, but he had nothing to say to her. Yet his eyes awoke her senses, her skin, and her femininity. Sometimes she felt angry about this sudden change and wanted to grab him and ask him the reason for his behaviour. She felt a sense of despair. All their childhood laughter had vanished; only echoes remained.

Elias's childhood was not that different from Laura's; the only difference being that both his parents were Lebanese. Yet despite their common origins, they never got along, and both lived two different lives, although Elias's father never gambled or left his wife. His mother, Nora, was the strong figure in the family; she was the only girl in a family of three brothers, from a village in the mountains. She was a very religious woman, prayed constantly, and rarely laughed. She saw modernity as a form of evil and believed that one was somehow closer to the truth with God at one's side. She was a typical Middle Eastern woman; each morning after cleaning the house, she would meet with her female neighbours and drink Arabic coffee; then they would all gather together for hours and talk about the future of their respective children in the coffee grounds. She was a very ambitious mother; she wanted one son to be a doctor and one to be a lawyer, but she knew that she had failed Elias. She often prayed to the Virgin Mary to guide him and take the anger out of him, as she could not reach him and found him very difficult to understand. His father was religious too—a simple man with no ambition at all. He loved playing backgammon with his friends. Deep down he was happy to see his wife taking care of the household. He listened to the news all day long, putting the radio very close to his ears to avoid interfering in the family business, especially when his wife and Elias were having an argument.

Elias was not particularly patriotic. Beirut for him was not so much a physical reality but rather a collection of memories, an idea that slipped through his mind to become a thousand stories and tales. He wondered sometimes if his father ever felt anything. Sometimes during the summer, Elias's father used to take both of his boys walking on hot sands barefoot, but he would never feel pain and remained silent. Their steps barely left any traces, only shadows in the sand, much like his father's impact on his life. The seemingly common religious faith offered a bond between his parents but could not obliterate cultural and social differences between their two personalities.

Elias's mother had a preference for his older brother who had been born with the umbilical cord around his neck. She almost lost him, but she prayed to *Mar Charbel* who saved him. The two brothers were totally different; her eldest was very cautious, careful not to upset his mother, open and funny while Elias did not care. He was a restless and rebellious child, shunned, excluded, and mysterious. He acquired a part in other stories just to forget his own fragmented story. He hated criticism and feared the unknown. Every day was a struggle. He dreamed of a space where he could think freely without being disrupted by differences—a place where he did not have to share the oblivion of death and a place where life was not lived with anguish, the fear of the unpredictable. Elias was a complicated character. He always tried to reduce otherness at every opportunity. Sometimes he was attracted by the obscure, the unspoken, and the inscrutable. His mother had a problem with him, or rather he had a problem with her. Something in her irritated him, so he failed to appreciate her even when she tried to be good to him. The only times he felt happy were when meeting with his childhood friends. They all lived in the same building as Laura, in an upper-class Christian neighbourhood. He came to visit his friend Mounir almost every day at sunset until 1982.

Elias was comfortable with Mounir because he did not ask any questions. He felt they were on the same wavelength, which gave him a sense of security in his unsettled world. Elias had a diary, but not for everyday events. He only recorded thoughts, emotions, and observations. He once wrote "I am looking for a world with shared communality with a mental map of predictability in this insecure world." He distanced himself from people he considered outsiders, those whose opinions he felt were sharply different from his own. He knew that most people were created by their surroundings, social contexts, and events in their lives, but in this respect Elias felt he was a lost soul, and he knew if he was not mindful of that he would be damned with no salvation. He didn't bother about his identity; how could he be troubled by such an abstract concept, especially when he knew he was doomed?

He was sixteen when he enlisted in the Christian militia. This was a turning point in his life. The war was at its height with daily car bombings in the Christian neighbourhood. Elias felt suddenly useful and took it as a personal call to protect his people. As the war stripped off happiness, staining the streets with blood and death, joy and innocence deserted Elias; little by little layers of sadness tinted his soul. He looked at Laura as an oddity especially when she wore her mother's 1950s' clothes due to the family's lack of money to buy her appropriate clothes. She amused him in a way. She was obviously different from any girl of her age. He didn't desire her, and yet he wanted her to be his. She was always waiting for him, sitting at the staircase, pretending to play hide-and-seek with her brother. One day during heavy bombardments, as she ran down the stairs towards the shelter, she bumped into him in his military uniform. He was holding a cigarette, going upstairs to meet Mounir as if nothing was happening.

"I am so afraid and terrified," she said, staring wildly at him.

His lip quivered; he looked at her and simply answered, "Oh, Laura, it will stop soon; don't worry."

She went on just staring at him. The sounds of bombing suddenly stopped. He became aware of background music instead, and for a long moment, neither of them said anything.

Then he said, "I like your hair…can I touch it?"

"Of course," she answered and felt the unspoken mutual understanding of how much they wanted to kiss each other. His fingers threaded themselves through hers; then he shook his head, biting down on his lower lip, and left the building.

He didn't even go up to see Mounir. He later wrote, "A kiss is a mark you leave behind; it shouldn't be a stain. Yesterday my commander asked me to be a sniper. I sat at the top of the building for hours and closed my eyes. I kept pulling the trigger, not seeing whom I was shooting. I felt relentless. I was a blind criminal, a killing machine. Today I couldn't wake up. I needed to hide under my pillow. I felt a river of blood surrounding my bed.

"How can I look at your beautiful eyes again, Laura? How can I kiss your soft lips?"

Elias became more and more involved in the war. His commandment sent him to fight on the demarcation line that divided Beirut into two zones, west and east.

He never complained. On the contrary he became addicted to daily violence. Thousands of people were displaced. Christian areas were besieged; medical supplies and water were running low. The war dragged on through 1981 with the occasional ceasefire. Elias's mood darkened until the only way he could tolerate the growing violence was to use drugs. Laura became a shadow to him, difficult to define. He once wrote in his diary, "I am considered a hero among the fighters. For them I cannot do wrong by killing the enemy. All I want is to sing and dance. All this has no meaning. Do you remember, Laura, how we used to throw buckets of water on the people passing by the building? They would scream at us, threatening to tell our parents, and Mounir would come out on the balcony all innocent. All this seems so far away. Now you dress like a grown-up girl with heels and lipstick while I have a gun and I kill people."

Chapter 2

IN THE MORNING of September 20, 1982, Elias came back home and left his rifle in the corridor. His mother rushed to greet him not knowing where he'd been. He looked at her with empty eyes, sat on the sofa, and almost melted into it to become part of an emotionless thing, used by everybody never asking or caring if they were too heavy, too rough, or how long they wanted to sit. He must have sat there for the whole night, as he only woke up the following morning when his father shook him to tell him to go to his room. He wanted to watch on the TV what had happened in the camps, but he didn't want to wake Elias up. Elias felt his body weighed a ton with its sinful load. As he passed the corridor to go to his room, the statue of the Virgin Mary looked different, as if she was looking at him, blaming him. How could he commit such horrendous acts on decent people, sacrificing them to the god of revenge, a black force promising him hell? He felt dizzy and dehydrated. He smashed the statue into a thousand pieces.

His mother came from the kitchen, howling and crying, "What's the matter with you? How dare you? Have you lost your mind?"

He seemed to react at the last sentence.

"Actually, yes, I have lost my mind," he said. He went over in his head the debate about whether what he did was moral or not; he argued with himself between self-punishment, disgrace, and justification of his acts. After all a soldier was expected to live or die, better to die with honour than live with the dishonour he had failed in his oath and surrendered. He had an instinctive need to justify his acts.

He screamed at her, "Do you have a problem with that? All my life you treated me like an imbecile compared to Tony. You're always putting me down even at your ridiculous morning coffee with George's mother. I heard you... actually last week...I heard you telling her 'I wonder if this child belongs to our family; he's so odd and silent. He really is a loser.' I hate you...I hate you, and I always will...You've ruined my life with your pathetic ambitions for me to be a doctor or a lawyer...I hate you as you always compared me to Tony because he is at the USJ, but don't forget that I have protected you from these scums of Palestinians. I protected all this fucking neighbourhood. Next time when you have your ridiculous morning coffee, remind George's mother that I allowed it to take place by keeping you all safe."

His mother was livid. She turned to his father who buried his head in his newspaper and pretended he hadn't heard anything. He knew Elias was right; his mother was always humiliating him.

"You hypocrite! Instead of saying anything, how can you let our son speak to me like that! What did you do all your life apart from playing cards and backgammon with your friends and leaving your son in the militia. You never had any ambition for yourself, let alone for your sons; you are a loser too," she shouted at her silent husband.

Elias left the house to seek out his friend Mounir.

⊷⊶◉ ◉⊷⊶

At the sound of heavy gunfire, Elias looked at the buildings lit up by fire. He didn't remember how long he stood there, gripping Mounir's hand so tightly that he lost all feeling, as if this was his last good-bye.

If Laura knew then that it would be the last time she would see him, she would have stayed on the balcony forever. As the firing spread, her mother ran out on the balcony, grabbed Laura's hand, and started screaming. There was chaos in the streets as people ran to the shelters.

Elias returned home, packed his clothes, and, without any good-bye, left to sleep at Mounir's. He turned for the last time to see that the door was closed and the breeze blew a red curtain out through a broken window. For a moment he was that broken window; the drama of the moment was inescapable. He couldn't face his parents anymore. He was tired of the constant arguments with his mother; her constant presence in the house was unmistakably a dissonant note of melodrama in his loneliness. She always said the same thing: "We should ascribe authority over all affairs to God." What about the earthly affairs he once asked her. He purposefully set out to challenge her constant parochial understanding of the world. She insisted that God provided the framework within which all our earthly matters are understood and dealt with. Her obsession with religion was a constant reminder to him of his sins.

Now he felt dirty; never in his life had he felt so filthy with the dried blood on his forearms. His father saw it when he shook him and knew what had happened. His father was ashamed but did not say a word to his son. Maybe he thought that Elias had fallen too low and there was no salvation or any way to bring him back. Elias was thankful to his father; he felt there was a kind of male understanding and complicity. He went down and bought a bottle of water to clean his arms and his shame in the street, and then he dragged himself up again to see Mounir. He asked apologetically if he could stay for few days, and Mounir accepted with some hesitation as his sister Neyla was still at home and said jokingly, "If you touch my sister, I will kill you."

Elias stayed there for two days, sleeping on the sofa, and then decided to leave Lebanon forever, vowing never to come back to this land or to his parents. He boarded the ship to Cyprus and the first stage of his journey to Brazil and his final destination, his uncle's coffee plantation.

→⊷⊷ ⊶⊷←

Once on the ship, he took the cheapest cabin with no view at all. The rocking of boat made him very sick. He couldn't sleep although he wanted to, but the noise from men playing poker and the smell of cigars made it impossible. The noise was so appalling that he left his cabin and went up to join the boys. People started chatting to him, asking why he wanted to leave Lebanon and where was he going. His answers were was vague and brief. He left the poker game and went out onto the deck. The wind was howling, and the waves were crashing against the boat. Through the spray, he saw a girl looking at him. He could not see if she was crying or wet from the sea, but her eyes looked right through him. She seemed sad, and he approached her.

"Hello."

"Hi."

"What are you doing here in this storm?" he asked.

"Looking at the lights of Beirut disappearing; when they do I'll go down and sleep…"

"Did you leave someone you love behind?"

"Oh yes…" she started crying. "My boyfriend. But my dad decided we should leave."

"Why he didn't come with you?" he asked her.

"Oh, he can't afford it, although I begged him to come. I would have paid for him, but he is very proud."

"Sorry to hear that. Was he in the militia?" he asked nervously.

"Oh no. He is an only child. I wouldn't have accepted it if he was after what those thugs did."

"What did they do?"

"The killings in the Palestinian camps. Haven't you heard about it?"

"Oh yes, briefly…" he tried to light his cigarette, but the wind prevented him.

"And what do you do?"

"First year law at the University of La Sagesse."

"So why are you here then?"

"My uncle lives in Brazil, and I've decided to go there. Apparently there are gorgeous girls there." He looked at her more closely; she looked very pretty with her frizzy hair playing with the wind.

Suddenly a voice called, "Maya! Maya! Can you come down immediately?"

"Oh, that's my dad—bye."

"Bye. Oh, if you can, I'm in cabin number thirty four—please try and come."

"Why? To do what?"

"Just lie down with me and talk. Please. Please."

He went down half an hour later and sat in his room, waiting for her to come, and he fell asleep in his clothes when a knock on the door woke him up.

"Who is it?"

"It's Maya. Open quickly; I can't stay more than few minutes."

He opened the door, and the next thing he knew, Maya was in his arms. He started kissing her violently until she moaned and calmed him down. He grabbed her hands and took her to his bed.

"I am virgin…"

"I'll be very gentle; don't worry."

After an hour they heard a voice in the corridor.

"Maya! Maya! Where are you?"

She put her clothes on and ran from the room, and he was left with her perfume all around him. He groaned and went under the sheets naked. He felt relieved and happy.

Once the ship arrived in Cyprus, he looked for Maya but didn't see her. In the distance he saw the silhouettes of two people disappearing behind a cab. He grabbed his small case and queued for a taxi. In his heart he was as afraid as Theseus facing the Minotaur; if only the oracle would confirm his success, then nothing else would matter. What I am doing going to Brazil? he asked himself. Why Brazil? I don't even speak the language. Now he missed his mother and the old man with his radio, the image of clothes hanging from the balcony, the neighbour's cat, the pastoral innocence of his childhood, and the sadness of Laura. He thought of her with a strange feeling. He never really loved her, but he was always intrigued by her—by her long insisting look, the way she walked or talked. She was so shy; she used to look at him for hours from her balcony. He knew each time he came to the building that she would be there like an icon attached to his chest. Her frizzy black hair always hid her small face. His torment and the lingering guilt never left him—they were constantly opening the gap between his innocence and criminality. He tried to find reasons to convince himself of the nobility of the task, but he failed. Laura was a reminder of his innocent world. She was intact, uncontaminated by these lower instincts, yet she was still unknown, mysterious, and terrifying. Innocence and criminality were antithetical, yet Elias tried to link them and to put the ultimate blame on the victims, but he was only fooling himself. His criminality was immutable.

He had instigated the massacre out of frustration. All his life he'd been second best to his brother's achievements. He had to prove himself worthy. When his parents stopped boasting about his elder brother, they seemed to remember him as a moving spirit, with his lifelike Chinese shadow puppetry. While his parents had a difficult marriage, they kept a certain civility in front of their two boys. His mother stood beside her husband and struggled with him through some terrible years and supported him through many ups and downs. Yet beneath this glittering display of family unity, things were broken.

Head down, shielding his face from full view with blood scattered all over his shirt and face, he walked slowly with his rifle in the narrow streets of the camps. He was silent, looking at the mud with shame, avoiding his comrades so that nobody could read his face and so no eyes could scan him. Everywhere around him his companions were cheering as if they were scripting a victory, but he refused to talk, nodding with his head when asked if he was proud of his actions.

Chapter 3

ELIAS BOARDED A flight to Brazil and arrived in Rio. His estranged uncle was waiting for him with a sign saying Elias Badawi. His uncle was another example of someone who compared his own prosperity to other people's misery. His name was Joseph; he was called *Giuseppe de la fiesta* in Brazil. He was an exuberant and uninhibited communicator. He was straight backed in his thin shirt, unshaven and ebullient although his soft expressive eyes looked tired. He was a tall, impressive man, with a proud bearing. He wore a white shirt with a wide collar, dark trousers, and a huge hat. He owned a vast coffee plantation, and local legend said that he needed a whole day on his horse to tour his lands. He was well connected, but many of his connections were shady, controversial politicians. He had lived quite alone for about the last eighteen years of his life, too busy for a wife; he had occasional sex with his maids. He fabricated tales about his life that travelled all the way back to his village in Lebanon. It was said that he'd been saved from an illness that almost killed him by a small piece of the cross of Christ an old friend had brought him from Jerusalem. When Elias's father lost his job during the civil war, Giuseppe was appalled at their impoverishment and sent them money to help. He was the rich man of his village and powerful too. Sometimes he stood in for the priest, frightening children with his sermons; he helped widows, gave advice on political issues, and urged solutions for unemployment. He invested his fortune in his plantation and his horses.

Once he was settled in Giuseppe's black Jeep, Elias finally relaxed. His mind drifted far away until he felt unreachable.

"So?" Guiseppe's hand squeezed Elias's thigh. "Welcome to Rio! We have a five-hour journey; you can relax and sleep if you want. I can't put the seat back because it's broken, but don't worry—just relax."

The old Jeep was not comfortable, but that was the least of Elias's worries. With the sleeve of his shirt, he wiped the grimy window and looked at the dusty landscape outside.

"Thank you," Elias said. "I'm fine. I need to rest. It's been a long journey in a boat…then a plane; it seems I was travelling forever." He wanted to go on in a sort of exile's lament but stopped himself and then with a sigh of relief said, "I am so lucky and happy to be with you! I couldn't wait to finally meet you. You're such a mythical character back home!"

Giuseppe laughed. He adored compliments, but Elias did not hear what his uncle was saying. He was struggling to find his voice, to find a compromise between his feelings and distinct realities. He was still searching among the discourses with their pros and cons, his emerging feelings, for his identity and relationship with the world around him. He didn't care about his uncle or where he was. He needed to leave his body and his soul and to look for another existence and another soul. He needed a place where he could become someone else.

Exile was good for Elias as he needed to recentre himself—to recreate meaning in his life in the new world that he was experiencing. He needed to open up new spaces for memories, as he seemed to have used all his capacity for memory. It was impossible for him to translate his history and experience to his new life. He had gone beyond a threshold, and any other sin would seem trivial by comparison. Everyone was purer than him. He was the only one contaminated; he couldn't deliver or admit his burden to anyone, not even to his uncle, this tough guy.

There were no cars along the broad sandy roads and only a few people walking in lockstep under umbrellas to shield them from a burning sun. Elias's thoughts were scattered, and his soul was withering. He wished his threshold for self-deception was lower so he could delude himself and feel innocent again. What should he do next? He had already threatened his mother that his absence would last for years.

"I have never stopped you from leaving!" she once cried. "Go whenever you like; maybe you should so you would appreciate me more…"

"Thanks to you I am drifting around in vain here," he shouted back. "I'm paying for it with my freedom and my useless loyalty! It's because I don't want to leave you that I'm stuck here listening to your nagging every day!"

"The road to hell is paved with good intentions," she answered. "You're impetuous, easily deceived; your altruism brings tears to my eyes, but you have no kindness towards your family. We did everything for you and—"

He interrupted her. "Yes…and your brother. 'I gave up my life and studies just to bring you up.' I've heard you say that a thousand times. Aren't you bored banging on the same drums all these years? Which studies anyway? Grandpa didn't want you to go to university—he wanted Uncle Giuseppe to study; he was happy that you got married and relieved too since you nagged him as well."

"No point discussing anything with you. Such a pity! What have I done to have a son like you?"

"You must have not prayed at *Laylat al-Qadr* properly," he mocked her and left.

He was sleeping in the car, but his sleep was agitated. He felt his uncle's hand on his face when he woke up and aggressively tried to ward off Giuseppe's soft hand. Giuseppe looked shocked at Elias's terrorized red eyes staring at him.

"Are you OK?" he asked. "You were moaning and sweating. I just wanted to be sure you didn't have any fever—you looked really unsettled."

"Yes…I'm sorry; I didn't realize…I was just dreaming…hah! I'm OK now. Did I sleep long? I mean how many hours."

"Oh, not long—maybe forty minutes or so, but you were saying weird things, that's all."

"Er…like what? I mean what things."

"I don't know; nothing very coherent—things like 'Kill them…you bitch… leave me alone…'"

"I see. Sorry; bad dream. Kill who? Ha-ha. I never even killed an insect. You know this war is terrible."

"I know, but we all have a war inside of us. Don't get me wrong. I'm not being snobbish, but here I fight every day with people who want to take my land.

I always bribe the weak to expose the strong—not a very orthodox method, but this is my land, and I worked hard for it."

Elias nodded and then turned his head to look at the landscape running past them. Trying to grasp and keep a memory of it was a race against time and speed. The sun was dipping behind the line of trees in the distance at the edge of the landscape. Instead of scanning the empty road, he looked up at the sky.

Elias quietly asked what he would do on the farm.

"Now what was agreed with your father? You'll be looking after the land. A hard job, but I need someone I can trust."

After a while, they finally reached the farm. Facing them was a long road bordered with trees, which led up to a big hacienda. As they slowly drove up to the house, men working on the land left their tasks and quietly stepped forward to greet them. Entering the big hall, Elias saw that the walls were shelved to the ceiling and filled with books and magazines. The blackened colonial floorboards were mixed with Portuguese *azulejos* ceramic tiles. Colonial period copper and bronze objects were scattered around the room, and above the central fireplace hung a big portrait of Giuseppe as a master surrounded by black workers ploughing the fields. On the left, down some stone stairs, was a lower terrace garden leading to the canal, which marked the boundaries of the main estate building.

A black woman appeared through the door and announced that dinner was ready. "Sir? Your favourite dish has been served in the dining room." Giuseppe answered distractedly that they would eat, but not now. She grimaced, looked away, and then hesitated before leaving the room. He ignored her and asked Elias to follow him as they made their way down the bank.

"Do we conquer in order to survive?" asked Giuseppe.

"No, I disagree," replied Elias. "We conquer for greed and power."

"It doesn't surprise me that you think that way. You're still very young. How old are you? Eighteen? Nineteen?"

"What has this to do with age?" Elias though and shot him a dark look but realized that he should consider before answering and not contradict his uncle again if he wanted to stay here. Clearly he was the master while they were here together. Elias was touched to see more workers saluting his uncle and then getting back to work. Giuseppe bent over, took some sand in his hand, and then straightened up breathing slowly.

"This is your dignity; your land is your existence. If you look after it, it will look after you well. You'll be replacing Danielo. He passed away from bone cancer last month—maybe due to malnutrition, I don't know, but he was very stoic about it. I'm short of strong muscles, and you seem to me the perfect replacement. You know, Elias, you are a puzzle to me. You had the nicest parents, so what made you leave Lebanon? Look, you shouldn't feel bad about your parents. Don't look back—anyway it is your business, young man. I'm here just as guidance. I own as far as you can stretch your eyes, and one day it will be all yours. I'm not married and won't marry anytime soon. I still have my legs and a joyful enthusiasm, but you will breed like rabbits—here the girls are very hot, and they won't spare you."

Elias shook his head. We're all victims in this world, he thought. We're all stuck in our dreams and in our head, and we can't escape. What can we know? Giuseppe hurled a stone and then turned and headed off back towards the house, striding through the bare landscape.

"We must get back for dinner!"

Elias turned to follow him and saw that Giuseppe had a gun tucked into his waistband.

"Why do you carry a gun, Uncle?"

Giuseppe stormed into the house, pretending not to hear, and sat at the table and shouted, "Sol, Sol, pour the wine!"

As the days passed, Elias had to deal with Giuseppe's mood swings. Elias lost the illusion that this was a new world for him. The harder we work, the weaker we become, he thought. Yet it was a form of healing, a self-punishment, his own salvation, and a way to purify his soul. There was something deserving in his suffering. Maybe he would meet the same fate as Danielo.

Every morning after drinking coffee, he pulled on his working boots and headed to the plot. Working the soil was like unearthing himself—deeper and deeper, the earth would break down to make the soil smoother. When the soil beds started bearing the first crops, it made him very happy at first, but then it all become dull like him. Nobody cared about his achievements or victories; gazing at the horizon was the only thing he could do. We all share the same oxygen, so what makes us different?

Elias felt that his choices were wrong and that he kept on being pushed through doors into rooms he didn't want to enter. He couldn't go back to the past. He later learned from another worker that guns were important for survival, and they had to be vigilant all the time.

"We're in a rural area coveted by thieves; never let anything out of your sight! Your uncle has already shot a thief in his house, but he missed him."

It was very tiring to look constantly over his shoulder. Yet strangely at the limit of all this chaos, things started to gain meaning for him.

The foreman gave Elias a piece of land and some tools, a scythe and a sickle. His life was dust and heat. He worked steadily every morning and then took a break at lunch, eating what the maid had prepared for him and finishing around 5:00 p.m. Working the land was the most honourable thing a man could do, Giuseppe once told him.

"When I came to Brazil, I worked very hard like you before I could afford to buy my first parcel of land."

Elias did not comment. He needed to lose himself, to forget his existence as a divine punishment that he had to fulfil in order to cleanse his guilt. Things were headed to a new beginning, but soon the illusion spread like dust and disappeared. Sitting there outside the shed, the stone walls around him became his prison. He could breathe his sweat, and with it came bad memories; he began to feel awkward and uncomfortable. One morning after hauling rocks, he sat in the shadow of an oak tree, sipping his coffee, and then he walked through an alley of trees and saw a squirrel. He felt the rough ground under his long boots. After strolling for a while, he heard two men chatting; he approached them from the side and saw it was Giuseppe talking to the governor.

"I bribed you enough for you to turn a deaf ear to all these rumours," Giuseppe said with twitching lips.

"What was enough in the past is not so now," said the governor. "My luck changed, and I've lost investments lately."

"So I have to pay for your loss?"

"Choose that, or they'll put you in prison."

"If I go down, I will make sure you go down with me," said Giuseppe angrily.

"No need to escalate matters. I'm just asking for a bit more. Look you're making a fortune here selling your coffee beans. Ten percent is not that much; then if you need any favours, I'll always be here for you. Nothing will change. We'll resume our business as before. Do you remember those days?"

"Yes, I do. I made you a governor when you were nobody…look, ten percent is a lot. I have wages to pay."

"To whom? To your nephew? He's working as a slave. I doubt you pay him."

"That's none of your business," said Giuseppe.

"OK, fine; just prepare the money. I'll come tomorrow to collect it," the governor snarled and left. Giuseppe saw Elias looking at them with a hard suspicious stare.

"How long have you been here? Who taught you to listen to people's conversations? Weren't you supposed to be working?"

Elias replied, "Long enough to know that you are in some kind of trouble."

"I'll handle it," said Giuseppe. "Please get back to work."

Elias took a long pause. "Yes, you're right. I'd better get going," he said. Then he raised his eyebrows. "Will you give him the money?"

Giuseppe turned his face away. "I don't make rules here," he said quietly.

Elias went back slowly to where his tools sat in a pile; with each step he took, he felt sadness and disappointment. There's no difference for me between this life and this land; they're both inactive, dead, he thought. Somebody needs to revive it, to work it over. But he could not do it alone anymore; he had run out of tools.

Chapter 4

THE SOUTH WIND picked up, bringing dust with it. Elias stopped ploughing and sat on a rock in the middle of the field He pounded his fist on the coarse surface, making it bleed. From far off he heard the noise of a car, which was a bit unusual at this time of the day. The delivery of food was always in the morning, he thought. He followed the car with his eyes and saw an elegant white silhouette get out of the car.

What's going on here? he wondered. He took two stones in his hands and walked towards the house. He saw the back of a woman wearing a big white hat. He coughed to attract her attention. She turned and introduced herself as Sally Gibbs, hesitating before she approached, and stared at him. He gulped, took a deep breath, and tried to calm himself. He felt unsteady and embarrassed in his bulky overall.

"Are you staying with us?" he asked.

"Yes, I am here for few days. I can't stay more," the woman said.

"Took me a while to get used to it too."

"It is Elias, I guess? Are you happy here? Do you feel at home?" she asked.

What a strange question, he thought. He shook his head. "I have no choice." He pretended not to hear the third question, and then he thought this place was definitely not home; it was death.

"So how do you know him?" He was careful not to let his eyes linger on her face.

"We're old friends."

He slapped the two stones against each other and then put them in his pocket. He did not say a word, looking at her lean face and big lips. Her white coat flapped open, and he saw her transparent white shirt. It had a golden trim along the breasts.

His uncle appeared through the front door. Mrs. Gibbs looked towards him and smiled. Giuseppe eyed Elias suspiciously.

"Hope you offered her a cold drink," he said as he approached.

"Oh no, sorry; we've only just been introduced."

"Ah. Manners, son. With beautiful ladies manners come first."

The workers gathered their tools, trailing out of the fields and walking in silence like ghosts as if their souls had been stripped from them. Giuseppe yelled at them to move faster as if they were blotting the landscape in front of Mrs Gibbs. Elias held on to his stones and apologized, "I'll come back later. I need to shower." Her presence seemed to push back the gloom from the big mansion.

⊶≡◉ ◉≡⊷

After his shower he selected a nice outfit and went down to the living room. The night air was thick and humid. Mrs. Gibbs took her coat off, revealing a pretty figure dressed in a blue silk skirt. She held a glass of red wine. He sat against the wall near the big window, looking at the dimly lit garden with a few rusty lanterns hanging from the trees.

Giuseppe joined them. He approached with an imperious expression and a self-assurance that annoyed Elias. His attitude conveyed the assurance that he was the master of the place and everybody else was of lesser importance. Elias felt a stirring inside of him. He wanted to be alone with her without having to share her with this arrogant old man. He covered a grimace and headed towards the table. Sally followed him and took a seat, tapping her finger on the arm of her chair and staring at the huge grilled fish laid out on a platter in the centre of the table.

"Well," Giuseppe said, "you've made me a very happy man! You have honoured my house. How is the hotel business going?"

"Good; lots of work, but I'm enjoying myself. The setting is great. You should bring Elias one day. It will do him good to get away from this heat."

"It won't happen before the end of the year. Lots to do here, and I need him." Giuseppe answered in an irritated tone, scratching his shaggy unwashed hair. He tossed the remaining gulp of whiskey down his throat.

Elias wanted to scream but restrained himself and fought hard to keep himself from shaking. How could someone decide his life for him? He longed for freedom, but he couldn't grasp it yet.

The serving woman disappeared into the back, and the smell of Giuseppe's cigar filled up the room, the smoke curling up from his mouth. Glancing around uneasily Giuseppe said, "Well then, we'll arrange a trip to see your hotel." Raising his eyebrows, he asked, "Eh, Elias? Would you like that?"

Sally interrupted before Elias could answer. "Come before my daughter's anniversary," she said and tried to cover the swell of grief that rose in her and blinked her eyes rapidly, taking a deep breath. "So, Elias, do you have siblings?"

"Yes, one brother, but we are not close. So you lost a daughter, I presume?"

Giuseppe sent him a dark look, and his fingers visibly trembled. Then relieving Mrs. Gibbs from answering, he suggested they have some drinks. Elias accepted the suggestion, as he wanted Giuseppe to relax again. Elias retrieved a flask of bourbon and offered Mrs. Gibbs a shot, which she accepted gladly.

Sally looked at his eyes and studied him quietly as he approached her. She found him handsome, irresistible.

"So what about a girlfriend then? Do you have one?"

He frowned. "No, not yet; she won't last here anyway. It is far from civilisation here."

"Perhaps you have one but prefer to keep her for yourself," she said, touching her short auburn hair and her sensuous lips.

"I would prefer not at the moment." His smile widened but not with warmth. His stare was flat and grey; there was something hiding under it. Suppressing a sigh, she understood that pushing him more could backfire on her. She turned to Giuseppe. "How are the politics going?"

"Not that easy; now we have elections coming soon. Ronaldo should be elected; he's on my side, but now it seems more and more difficult to achieve it, especially with the lack of safety here."

"Yes, I heard it was bad; you almost killed someone?" She eyed Elias over the rim of her glass. "Elias, do you carry a gun? You should be careful here." She tensed, and then she softened again.

"He refused!" Giuseppe said angrily. "He thinks himself an immortal hero."

"Well, my life ended some time ago, so who cares what could happen now?" he said, sipping his neat bourbon.

"What do you mean?" asked Mrs. Gibbs. "How has your life ended when it has barely commenced?"

"That's Elias for you; everything has an answer!"

In a soft voice, Sally added, "We all have tragedies." She glanced away with a hint of sadness in her eyes. "Life is a gift."

Giuseppe went to the black Chinese cupboard, retrieved a lacquered box, opened it, and there was a gun. It sat on a red velvet casing. "This is yours. I want you to have it," he said, pressing the box into Elias's hands.

Elias stepped forward. "Why give it to me now?" He suspected it was a gesture made to impress Mrs. Gibbs.

"Why not now?" Giuseppe asked.

Mrs. Gibbs forced her eyes to meet his and then muttered, "You should defend yourself. Here people are very poor."

Elias took a long breath. His face turned pale and red; he trembled, and his eyes rolled up. His voice became weak, and he stared speechlessly at his uncle. Then he lost his lucidity and collapsed.

--->=== ===<---

The next morning he woke up in his room, not remembering anything from the previous night. He looked at the small round clock near his bed; it showed 10:00 a.m. He jumped from his bed and went downstairs when he saw Sally leaving Giuseppe's bedroom, half naked, wearing only a white transparent robe.

"How do you feel?" she asked.

"Still feel weak."

She pulled her hair back, showing a very sensual neck; she wanted him to kiss her. He considered all the options carefully and then glanced around just to make sure that he was alone. H moved towards her and grasped her hands. Her palms were hot, her chest was rising and falling, and he could see her nipples.

"What do you want from me?" he glanced at her with confusion.

"Make me happy," she answered.

"Don't count on me for your happiness—if I have the power to give it to you, then I can also take it away."

He wrapped his hands around her waist and kissed her on her neck; stripping off her robe, he pushed her nipples inside his mouth, biting them. A pinched smile replaced the full one that had graced her face earlier. She wanted him to make love to her there on the stairs and didn't care about Giuseppe. She never allowed him inside of her, but with Elias things were different. He flung her down on the step, and without speaking he climbed astride her. And it took him two minutes to reach his climax. He continued kissing her, and she whipped back her sweaty hair. Then suddenly he pulled her robe back as he heard a gasp. She ran away towards the bathroom. The bedroom door opened, and Giuseppe appeared sweaty and bruised but very happy. He looked at Elias and felt immobilized; Elias could feel a suspicion in his eyes.

"What the hell happened to you yesterday? Did you see the time? It's almost ten thirty; you should have been in the field and having your morning break by now."

"I'm sorry." He caught her eye, and she offered him a glance of silent support before storming away to the bathroom. Late in the afternoon, Elias joined her in the drawing room, and they shared a whisky, albeit in heavy silence. She didn't draw away from him, and he felt a connection beyond the physical one. She was much older than him, and yet he needed her.

"I'm leaving tomorrow morning," she said quietly.

He looked at her with an unreadable expression. "Then things will be different tomorrow." Bumping her shins against the chair, she winced a moment in agony.

"Wish you could come with me," she said.

He wiped the sweat from his brow, and breathing steadily, he stood up. "I can't, Sally. I can't. He is my uncle after all."

Sally peeled the label from the whisky bottle. She felt elated and crushed at the same time. "So I can't see you again; this is our last moment," she said and then retired to her room.

Giuseppe appeared moments later, and Elias's heart started beating fast, anxious that his uncle might have seen something. He changed topic and started talking and chatting politics, blinking sweat out of his eyes. Giuseppe seemed very serene, compared to his earlier sadness, after a long shower, trying to wash his growing anxiety. Unbidden tears erupted when he looked at his tired body in the mirror of his large black-tiled bathroom. "Oh, don't worry, young man, about pleasing me. I know politics is not your cup of tea. Anyway what do you think of Sally? She seems to really like you."

"Yes, she is a nice woman, but are you in love with her?" Giuseppe averted his eyes. "I've known her forever, and I suppose it must be love."

"Why didn't you marry her then?"

"Ah well, not every story has to end in marriage. She had her dramas, and I had mine. Now she's free but still…"

Tasting something bitter on his tongue, Elias replied, "She seems to show a lot of dignity in a graceful way."

"You mean following her daughter's death?"

"Yes; I don't know how she does it. I couldn't have lived such a tragedy, such a death."

"I would do anything to help her, poor soul."

Elias took a long deep breath and occupied himself with moving the two drinking glasses, touching the rim where her lips had touched the side of the glass. "Death is terrible and unfair, uncle, but this is life!"

Chapter 5

ONCE ELIAS HAD left, Laura felt she had no choice but to travel. The law university became a burden. Even this was her father's choice. She wanted to enrol in fashion design but wasn't allowed.

"You want to become a tailor who does men's suits"? he once shouted at her.

"No, this is art," she replied, "and has nothing to do with men."

Lebanon had become a dead end. She had no voice in her family, and she wasn't allowed to express herself or define her own sense of being. She could stop her journey but not indefinitely. She felt like a soldier abandoned in the war zone—helpless. Her life was written by other people; she could not stand her father with his radio all day long, nor her brother following her and spying on her, nor the political discourse of her mother. It seemed that everything had been tolerable because Elias, in one way or another, was part of her life, but now it was time to move on.

Laura's father was a big advocate of protecting virginity. Virginity in the Middle East seemed to be more of a male concern than a female one. The fear of losing it could be prompted by a suggestive look or a harmless chat with a stranger. He pointed out to her the importance of the people around her and that she should learn how to please them before pleasing herself. He would often say, "I know more than God." He loudly mocked the Nietzschean vision of the world that said the world was our making with no definitive truth. Laura also believed that there was no universal truth; the world depended on our language for its existence, so then a multilingual world implied multiple perspectives. So if our world is subjective, then it was her own right to view the concept of virginity as she wished. Only those who lived at the periphery of the social order needed guidance through traditions to teach them how to perform their role in society.

Once her father slapped the newspaper on the table where she was having her breakfast. "Even in Roman times, the vestal virgins had to remain virgins for thirty years. These six handpicked priestesses had to tend the perpetual fire at the temple of Vesta. After their service they were allowed to marry, but very few did. So you see your virginity should also be sacred! By the way don't look at me like this. Even the Welsh poet Ivor Novello mentioned virginity in his famous poem "keep the Home Fires Burning" in 1944.

Laura could not stand this male discourse; she refused to be like thousands of women who were forced to tend the fire of passion in a man's heart and her own heart in the temple of love before she could sacrifice her virginity on the pyre of decency and honour. She was not prepared to do that. Her life was a sacred journey, which she intended to celebrate with expressions of joy, love, and passion. In her view "sacrifice" was the only word that should be taken out of the dictionary, as it was always followed by resentment.

Laura met Philippe who worked at the French consulate in Lebanon. He was a Frenchman with a gentle soul—a tall man with blond hair and blue eyes. When she presented her passport for a visa, he started chatting to her and then asked her if she wanted to meet up sometime for coffee.

They met in a quiet café in Achrafieh. Laura arrived almost an hour early and hid herself in a corner. Philippe arrived and came towards her with a quick, sprightly stride.

"Ah, here you are! I was looking everywhere for you. Sorry I'm late. I had some admin stuff to do," he said as he sat down.

He wore casual clothes, which Laura thought matched the warmth he expressed through his slightly protruding eyes. She was struck by his attentive apology as in fact he was only two minutes late.

"How are you?" he boomed. "Ready for some coffee and a talk?"

He chuckled, obviously in a good mood. He was smiling, and nothing seemed to worry him.

"Have you been here for some time?" he asked, suddenly looking concerned.

"No," she lied, "I just arrived. Do you think I will get my visa?"

"I can't disclose such matters, but we look at each applicant separately. Why do you want to leave so much?" he asked, glancing quickly round the café. Laura looked impatient. Her eyes too looked round the neighbouring tables. Why does everybody ask me the same question? she thought.

"Why not?" she retorted.

She felt the weight of his hand on hers. "Isn't there a more private place where we could discuss this?" he asked.

Her heart started beating. "Please, no public display of affection; this is Lebanon."

He swiftly removed his hand and apologized. "Sorry, I didn't mean to, but I like you a lot—something in your eyes I like."

Suddenly he looked tired despite his earlier show of energy. "Would you care for anything? A Lebanese dessert maybe?"

"No, I'm fine; now I have to go."

"Please don't. Come with me…"

He raised his hands to her passive face and then to her shoulder. With her eyes shut, she felt the urge to kiss him.

"OK," he said. "I'll take you to my house."

She accepted and soon found herself on the floor of his kitchen. He was on top of her, and all she could see was the soft-green foliage and hovering kingfishers painted on the ceiling. Her face was red, irritated by his unshaven beard. But he was very gentle and aware of her state, so she felt neither pain nor pleasure.

She spoke in his ear, "How much time has passed?"

Her face remained calm with a childish expression. He looked at her and then looked away, and after a while she pushed him off her body very slowly and made her way to the bathroom, blood dripping along her thighs. Thoughts ran round her head, thoughts of no importance; they were fragments of a dream she tried to piece together.

How did it feel? she asked herself. And was it worth it? She didn't, however, feel happy or afraid. She felt like an outside observer.

"Hey," he said. "Do you want a glass of red wine to celebrate? Well, as they say you are a woman now."

He was probably anticipating his next meeting with her, she thought. She sent him a hard stare, and he blushed slightly and turned away, clearly embarrassed by his crude words.

"Can you please excuse me? I need to shower."

"Yes, of course, Laura. Please feel at home."

In the bathroom in front of the mirror, she had a funny thought: I've just sacrificed my virginity. Suddenly her father's opinion didn't matter. It was her body, and this was her life, her decision. She felt vulnerable afterwards in front of him, lying on his back, looking through the window. Then she understood what virginity was about: it was a shield that a woman should keep as a protective amulet with the advantage of choosing to whom she would surrender it.

He put on his blue jeans and looked solemnly at her. She looked back worried; now that she'd lost her amulet, what would happen to her? She wondered if the spark of this moment would ever flare again. Somehow, somewhere, she knew she was leaving Lebanon soon and would probably never see him again. Would he remember her? The expectation of the future or its judgement of the past worried her. Predominantly this was an ethical issue for her. She hadn't done it for love—that she knew. She wanted to prove to Elias that a French guy found her attractive. Philippe stole what Elias could have had consensually on any of the long hot nights on the roof of the building.

--}==⊙ ⊙==}--

A week later Philippe called her at home. He asked to see her directly at his house. He liked her a lot, he said, and she'd become a chronic obsession. He wanted to make love to her again and again. He couldn't wait to leave the dusty overcrowded office and run home just to be with her. Philippe took her in his arms and asked her to stay in Lebanon so they could be together. She could not; it was too much to ask, she said. She had to construe her aim and her role in life. She told herself she had to fight against the hegemony of the values that she had just scrapped—the words and gestures of how a woman should behave in the presence of men. Like the bullfighter waving the red cape in front of the bull's

33

eyes and swinging to another side, each move has a meaning until he can stab the bull in the heart. This was the ultimate goal—a stab in the heart, and then the bull is all yours, like a man when he becomes yours like a ring in your finger.

Philippe was the kind of man who easily became desperate, and now he needed a reason to stay in Lebanon.

"Why do you want to stay here when all of us are leaving?" she asked him.

"It's the culture, the sun, and girls like you," he replied.

Despite his insistence, she found it very difficult to contemplate. How ironic. She was fighting for the love of someone she had known almost all her life, and here was a guy whom she'd met only a few weeks ago, who wanted her to spend her life with him.

"Culture? We write from right to left because looking at the past is inherent in our way we write and think. Every Arab or Persian poet liked to weep on the heap of bones left by the tribe of his beloved; an individual established a relationship with a particular place and so ground his identity in a mound. The connections between the individual and his kin are closely intertwined. Nothing looks towards the future in our culture; why would you want to live backwards?"

He laughed at her clearly thinking her mad or drunk.

"Why do you really like this culture?" she asked.

"I couldn't find happiness in Paris, so I had to find a new job in the foreign ministry. I chose Lebanon because of the political unrest, knowing that my application would be swiftly accepted. Of course Beirut being a mythical city with all that Phoenician, Greek, and Roman legacy made it a very appealing choice."

Laura found that so romantic and naïve. As she left his house, she realized Philippe was genuine, and his requirements were simple and clear. They oscillated around a healthy relationship. It was up to her to leave or stay, and that was a rather-complex decision. Her decision to leave was based on a series of assertions—her father was a tyrant, her mother totally submissive, and an absent love. Ownership was a quintessential element of her culture and very well embedded in Middle Eastern thought. She was bullied by her friends because her family never owned her their own home. It was possible that a deeply felt loss of ownership of a certain place and kinship might have been instrumental in her desire to leave. Elias may have triggered this sense of loss and made her move exponentially forward in her life. Before meeting Philippe, she felt she had to prove something to both her childhood love and father, but now after this encounter, neither mattered anymore; she'd grown from a girl to a woman.

She grabbed her scarf from her pocket, wrapped it around her neck, and walked out proudly. For the first time in her life, someone had given her back her body and identity. She was not the mirror of her society, conforming to what the neighbours might think. She did not belong to the people and the neighbours anymore; she was herself. What is wrong with that? she thought. After all we are all humans, and survival is quintessential to our condition. What's wrong with dancing naked when everybody expects you to keep your clothes on? What's wrong with endlessly singing the same old song when everybody wants you to be quiet? What's wrong with exposing yourself and your beauty when everybody else expects you to stay home and do nothing?

→→══◎ ◎══←←

The more Philippe wanted her, the more she resented his weakness and passion. One day in his stilted voice, he announced to her that her visa was finally ready.

"Isn't that a bit late? It took four months."

"Better to have it late than never. But you told me your father won't allow you to leave, so surely it doesn't matter?"

As he listened solemnly for her answer, she said hoarsely, "Can you repeat that please? It's your job to bring me the visa."

He replied harshly, "Yes, you're right. It's my job—no more, no less."

On the day of her passport retrieval, she saw his face behind the rectangular glass; he looked sad and defeated. He opened his drawer, not looking at her face, and handed her the passport. She asked to see him later in his house; she wanted a moment of eternity, power, and seduction.

In his bedroom she laid on her back. He kneeled and faced her, and they started embracing each other. He caressed her breast, kissing her nipples and going down to her thighs, licking her tummy and navel with passion and deep desire. He gently plunged deeper inside her vagina and then looked at her face, watching her expression as he was moving in and out. She hid her face in his shoulder and cried silently. He stopped and embraced her. She was here spreading her legs for him who was penetrating her and supplying her with everything she always wanted. She was sobbing, moaning with pleasure. To her he was weak but peaceful, grounded, and filled with certainty. She loved him but was fighting it, running away. His stress started melting away in his legs, and he came everywhere in her body. The future seemed a prison housing unconscious fear and hopeless desire to keep things the way they are. After they finished he suggested having a pot of tea, so she wrapped herself with the hot wet sheet. While he disappeared into the kitchen, on the bedside table, she saw a pile of papers scattered. She grabbed the first one on the top, expecting a random letter from the consulate and saw a registration form filled with his personal details. She read the name Philippe Brocourt, age twenty-nine, family status married, child only one...

She pulled herself from the bed, feeling her heart pounding through her chest. She ran to the bathroom and then on her knees started vomiting inside the cubicle. At the sound of her vomit, he tried to grab her, panicking when she started shouting and crying.

"You filthy liar, you're married with a child! You lied to me. How dare you? I gave you my virginity...do you know what that means for my father? And then you were begging me to stay with you in Lebanon. Are you out of your mind?"

He didn't reply; he looked ashamed. Then he pulled her close to his chest. She was in shock and shivering violently in his arms as if she was in the throes of a fever.

"Well...it doesn't seem that way...I don't love her anymore, but it's difficult to leave her...I understand. I'm sorry. I never meant to hurt you," he stammered. "I just couldn't let you go. What am I going to do now alone without you? Please don't leave me. I'm nothing without you. You are too idealistic, Laura! Life is not perfect."

He followed her to the bus stop, trying to beg her to stay, but she wouldn't listen.

-->=◉ ◉=<--

The bus dropped her a few yards from her house. It was over for her; she was angry with his twisted logic, his denial of reality. She would really have liked to keep him as a friend, but when a woman loves a man, she gives him a part of her, she thought, and this one doesn't deserve it! Walking down the street, the sound of her heels was loud and heavy, echoing the voice inside her, repeating itself, the same old sentence again! "No dignity! You never learn; always the same mistake. What is the point of being clever in school and stupid in life?"

Philippe was obviously hurt by Laura's decision. He tried to call her many times, but she didn't pick up the phone and told her mother not to answer either. She was aware that she had inherited the same character as her father. "Too black and white like your father; put some water in your wine," her mother used to tell her. But she couldn't. Not in this instance where she felt betrayed, or maybe deep down she didn't want to admit that her father was right. "Men are predators; be careful, Laura."

Chapter 6

THIS EVENT WAS the breaking point in her decision, finally, between staying in Lebanon and leaving. The shift was clearly towards leaving. In her history she could only think of one similar crisis—the day she nearly lost her father. At that time all objectives died when he was kidnapped by the Palestinians for a few hours and then released. She gazed in awe at his face appearing through the door of her room. She thought she would never see him again. He looked pale and tired, and she knew that if he had died, it would have meant the end of the household. Her understanding of her world without him suddenly had no importance; she existed only as a reaction to his existence, ideas, and experience. She understood that when she used to do something dangerous to prove a point to him, it was nothing compared to recognising the danger of losing him.

She was not that playful little girl anymore. She had reached an ultimate point of strength and weakness at the same time. She stopped telling lies to people just to see their response. That day she grew up in an instant.

Her father always used to ask her, "Do you love me?"

"Above the stars and the world, Dad," she would reply. "Until I am insane with love." She hated her mother and found her wicked. "I don't want to be like you!" she would shout at her mother. Unexpectedly, her mother nodded and said that this is why she should leave Lebanon and marry a foreigner.

It was as if violence and love had wrenched her from herself. She knew her inner longings; she wanted to obliterate herself in one brief but splendid moment. Life and death in Lebanon became one source of life. Ancient Egyptians lived for death and expressed this through art and monumental tombs. They desired eternity, and they knew that life was precarious. She knew it now too. War killed every ambition for life, and people lived through the death of others. Everyone was stuck in the same madness, but her father refused to leave.

"To die here in your country is the best death. You have to preserve your dignity wherever you are, Laura," he used to say.

"How can you see dignity in death? No coherence there, Dad. War is a source of unhappiness, and that is all. We are all too distracted to think about dignity. Why do people make a point of lying to you? It defies understanding and has the potential to hurt you. Why hide the ugly truth of war? What happens to you when you see a dead child lying in the street? How has war preserved his dignity? I believe what I see, Dad; it's part of you. Seeing is believing—you always taught me that. It's part of the story unfolding inside of you."

"On one hand we want to survive, help, and fight, but in order to do that, we have to stop being humans. Sometimes that entails killing, Laura; it's a struggle. Sometimes it's pointless, and sometimes it's essential—thinking and acting go together. Old assumptions seem meaningless, and new rules replace them. Each day is a new upheaval. We should learn to adapt, but never lose faith and hope."

"You say that, but you left Egypt, Dad."

"That's different. We all knew that we would lose, so there was no point in fighting. Now I am here, and I am not leaving, nor you. Do you see what I am trying to say? In order to live, you must die many times."

"Then die alone. I don't want to be part of this! Die alone…" she muttered.

But today she felt that by leaving Philippe, it was a death somehow: the death of her childhood, the death of love, the death of her virginity. The events were all blurry in her mind. What had really happened, and what had not? Slowly and steadily the city seemed to consume itself; the sun was setting. Her whole world was melting away just like the day. Minutes later she could hear explosions far away. No matter how often she heard these sounds, she could never adapt to them. She asked a shop owner about the news. He stared at her with a dumb expression, a stupid glare; he didn't know.

Walking the streets during bombings was dangerous as escape was not easy, but she needed to feel alive. If you cannot run and protect yourself, you may as well decide to stop breathing. Death can strike at any moment; it's unpredictable. You do not control your own fate; destiny controls you. Treachery and death swirl around you, hemming you in on all sides.

The streets were empty, and an old woman shouted at her to take cover. She managed to get shelter for few minutes, and then she ran to the house. She walked down the corridor and went to her room. She sat on her bed, feeling, empty and disgusted with herself. Nevertheless she had to maintain cheerfulness no matter how dismal the things that happened to her that day as her father could easily read her. She had her passport in her pocket, but he still did not know. There was so much she wanted to tell him but could not. She realized how little he understood her and her problems.

"Always do your best, Laura."

"But how, Dad? What do we mean by 'living'?"

"Laura, you can't ask these questions. Let us see when there is nothing, what do you think things would look like? A better life, yes? There is no meaning, no mission. We come, and we go; that's all. We don't have much choice. Some people call it life, some a journey, others a theatre; it doesn't matter."

"This is utter despair, Dad; there's so little left. We are not given a choice. Things are changing; look at our house: all the pipes are corroded, the wallpaper is falling, and we live in chaos. I feel I am asphyxiating. I really need to travel, Dad."

"Oh, all of this is because you want to travel; all this discourse about death is about this then, Laura?"

"What do you mean, Dad? War is a reality—stop reacting as if it wasn't!"

"It doesn't end here, Laura. We are still producing, eating, heating our houses, drinking, and laughing."

"No we are not, Dad! I am not. I feel dead. All my friends have gone; yours too, may I remind you."

"Well, that's it. I can't afford to move, and we will stay here whether you like it or not. Just grow up, Laura! Be grateful; other people have no houses anymore or parents."

There was no point in going further in the discussion, so she took a bath and went to bed. There were two wars—one outside and one inside her.

➵➾ ⬿➫

Laura sat eating a cheap meal in a restaurant overlooking the bus station. She shrugged at the idea that actually all her dreams were shattered. Her existence was plain, and she was tired of everything around her. It was impossible to be without Elias. She was tired of love and of chasing it. She lost confidence in herself and her abilities.

Days passed, and she would sit on her bed for hours looking at the ceiling or when it rained watching it from the rondos of her room. All she wanted was a phone call from Elias. He could take my number from the neighbour, she thought. But the phone never rang. Once her father caught her crying; he told her it is more difficult to be loved than to love. How does he have the answer to everything? she thought. It seems that parenting suddenly gives you the ability to see things that your children do not.

She caught her father once writing to his first love. He told her that he regretted leaving her just to save his pride. He was a sad man who never truly loved her mother. She always made a promise to herself that whatever happened, she would never be sad and that happiness would always be at her side.

"Happiness is only moments, Laura; tribulations far outnumber joys in life."

"Dad, if there are only moments, then by the time you've realized it, they are already gone," she answered innocently.

"Yes, that is kind of true, and this is why always live the present moment. When you think about something else, you miss that moment, and it is like you made a pact with yourself to never be happy."

"Could we not know these moments ever, Dad?"

"Life is full of surprises, Laura. Things are what they are, and we decide to interpret them differently. Like you love me with your mother, and you want us to love forever, but one day when we are old and very sick, you would want us to die just to relieve us from illness and suffering. It is hard for you to see it that way now, but later it will be your compassion that will judge."

"So when you and Mum are young, I owe you respect, but when you become older, I owe you compassion?"

"Yes, sort of, but it will be out of love. This is why life is precious; make it good, happy, and not full of regrets."

Regret—she wondered if she regretted the moment that she left Philippe. I cannot be dealing with Philippe's child, she thought, but will I ever find someone who will truly love me like Philippe?

"How can I be sure of a good future, Dad?"

"Fearing the future is fearing the unknown, and only mad people fear the unknown."

Laura hid the news of her passport. It was already July 1984, and Elias had left on September 21, 1982, yet it was like a century ago. She started avoiding her father more and more, and after their chess games, she would run to her room. She built a huge grudge towards him. She felt that he wanted to keep her in Beirut only out of selfishness. Her mother always said that all men were the same. She was right—Philippe, Elias, and her father. She could forgive both Philippe and Elias, but her father was different. Life was difficult at home with her mother depressed and shouting all the time for the bombs to stop. And her father always used an irritating voice when he met a different opinion to his own.

"Sin and temptation often happen, Laura. You should fight Satan and remain religious and virgin."

He read her mind and knew she did not care, which made him even more irritated but abandoned the hope of changing her views. She also felt a deep regret and started convincing herself that leaving was madness. What was she going to do alone in Paris? A university friend that she barely knew told her to come to Paris and that he would look after her. Her father's financial situation was abominable; they had lost everything during the war. Reduced to only one salary, she couldn't even dream of living abroad. Her father seemed to think that evil was everywhere outside the doorstep. His is an example of honesty, I guess, Laura thought, and maybe I can live through the war.

One day coming home from shopping with her mother, she found her brother in a state of total despair, crying uncontrollably. She tried to calm him. Her father was angry, shouting insults and threats at her brother. When Walid found his voice again, he told her that he had heard their father speaking on the phone and talking inappropriately to a young woman, trying to convince her to stay in Lebanon with him.

In the shocked silence that followed, a coin fell and rattled down the tiled floor in the living room, breaking the tension. Everyone stared at it. Laura grasped the moment and slipped quietly from the room to avoid the family seeing the look of triumph on her face. She knew this incident had propelled her dream of leaving Lebanon forward. She walked slowly into her room. In her desk drawer, she found her passport. She rushed to write a letter to Christian, a law student she met at her university. He left few months back and was occasionally sending her letters through his sister. She knew he liked her, and now he was her only hope, a kind of stepping stone that will take her to Elias. A knock sounded on the door, and her father entered, looking forlorn.

"You are too young to understand; it is not what it seems."

So her father, caught in the middle of a lie, tried to convince her that what she had seen and heard was not reality. She stood for a moment, her large dark eyes staring at him.

"Don't worry. I don't want or need to understand. I am leaving Lebanon; this is my passport, and this is my visa. Please could you book a flight to Paris for me?"

He took a cigar from his pocket. "So all this was done with your mother behind my back. When do you want to go? "

"Leave Mum alone; she has nothing to do with it."

"Don't tell me what to do."

Her father found something of value here and tried to make the most of it. "Sit down," he said awkwardly. "I paid for everything so far and gave you a decent life here with Walid and your mother. I sacrificed myself for this family."

She shook her head. She knew that leaving Lebanon depended on how guilty he could feel. She had to play it very carefully so as not to awaken the tiger inside of him.

"Why does it bother you if I leave?"

"I can read your mind," he said, looking defensive. "You are in love; you are not leaving here because of the war."

She raised her eyes and, confronting him, said in a low voice, "No, it is not true. I love Paris and also because of the historical ties between France and Christians."

"I see; so why Paris then? And where are you going to sleep?"

"Many of my girlfriends at the university moved there; surely someone will help me out at the beginning."

"OK. I will book the flight for Paris. MEA only go on Wednesdays and Fridays. Which one do you prefer? Oh actually, it is a discounted ticket, so we don't have a choice."

"OK. No worries. Any day is fine."

She smiled and leaned back, feeling like a general who had just won a battle. She caught an expression of bewilderment on his face as he left the room. The bewilderment changed to sullenness. He called her mother, and his voice faded out as he closed the door behind him. Then there was silence.

Her father had to face a tough choice: his wife or the mistress. It wasn't easy as all he cared about was his family. He sat in the balcony in despair and then fell asleep. He was awakened by the bark of a stray dog, lazily basking in the sun. He turned around and shouted at him. "You fool, you shouldn't have exposed yourself to ridicule when you had no means to protect yourself." Then defeated he buried his head in his hands.

Chapter 7

LAURA BOARDED THE flight to Paris on October 17, 1984. Her mother had managed to come to the airport to see her depart, and from a huge crowd, she saw a small hand waving at her; she waved back with tears in her eyes. She had nowhere to stay in Paris—only a piece of a paper on which her father had written to his distant cousin, a nun in a convent.

Arriving in Paris, she was met at the airport by her university friend, Christian. He walked towards her his arms outstretched. They embraced briefly. They had seen each other only a few months ago. He left before the final exams as had many of their friends. She had to wait until the summer where she failed her exams on purpose so she could have an excuse to leave Lebanon. Her jeans and thick sweater seemed out of fashion in comparison to his elegant summery outfit.

"I missed you," he whispered in her ear. She started feeling a growing emptiness, as his presence suddenly overwhelmed her; she was terrified.

"So where do I take you now?" he asked.

"I don't know; wherever." He saw her concern and heard her wary voice. Laura felt the last thing he wanted to do was to find her a room.

"What do you mean? You don't have any place to sleep tonight?"

"No," she answered.

"OK," he nodded. "I will find something; you are with me now, and that is all that matters."

They went straight to the car where Ramiz and Hassan were waiting inside.

"Hello, Laura. *Bienvenue* a Paris," Ramiz said, putting on a French accent.

"Hello, guys," she said, laughing back at him.

Christian suggested that first they should go to the *Brasserie Montparnasse* for a *cote de beouf*, and then he would deal with Laura's accommodation. They headed there with Ramiz flirting at every beautiful girl they saw.

"Hey, beauty, do you want to have dinner with us?" he called out several times.

Once inside the restaurant, Laura finally relaxed, still a bit overwhelmed but happy.

"So how is Lebanon?" Christian asked.

"Not that great. I am happy to have left—"

"Where are you staying?" Hassan interrupted her.

Christian intervened before Laura could find her words. "With me," he said, lifting his wine glass as he shot Laura a suggestive glance.

"Ah, OK; where exactly? At the boys' boarding house? You have to put her on the invisible clock then."

Laura looked surprised. "Why is that?"

"Ah, because it is only for boys; girls are not allowed to stay there."

"So what do you suggest?" asked Christian, clearly irritated by Hassan having the final word.

"Why not the girls' boarding residence? My aunt is a nun. I could speak with her now," Hassan said.

"OK," said Laura.

"How much would it cost?" Christian asked.

"I don't know. It's a ten-minute walk from here; we could all go after dinner if you want."

Christian wanted to spend the night with Laura; he was clearly irritated by Hassan's suggestion yet had no choice but to go along with his suggestion. They laughed and talked throughout the meal about university and teachers and their past.

"We have to throw a party for you," Hassan said with his usual laugh.

"That's all he thinks about in life—girls and parties," said Christian.

"What else is there?" asked Hassan.

After dinner they headed to the convent where Hassan spoke with his aunt who said Laura could stay for ten days while she looked for another alternative.

Laura agreed reluctantly, and Christian hugged her. "I will come to fetch you tomorrow morning; sleep well. I will deal with the cost; don't worry," he said as they parted.

Laura walked beside the nun through a long corridor into the convent. At the end of the corridor, the nun said, "Turn left, go to the second floor, and it's the first room on your right. This is your key; you will be sharing the room with another girl. Please walk quietly, as some girls might be asleep. Give me your passport, and I will photocopy it and give it back to you tomorrow."

Laura gave the nun her passport and went up. The first floor was the nuns' residence with a small chapel on the left. She walked on up to the second floor. She knocked on the door of the room; nobody answered, so she went in.

The room was a mansard—very simple with a vinyl-covered floor, two beds, two small wall cupboards, and a table with two chairs. She threw down her heavy luggage and lay down on a bed. This room needs more than paint! she thought, looking at the walls, but it's better than nothing. She shrugged. She unpacked some of her clothes, got into her pyjamas, and sank with exhaustion into bed. Hope my roommate is nice, was her last thought before she went to sleep.

The next morning the phone rang, and the receptionist told her that a boy called Christian was waiting for her downstairs. She rushed to get dressed and went downstairs to meet him.

"Here you are. So it wasn't a dream after all," he said as he kissed her and tenderly touched her hair.

"Yes, I am here," she smiled.

"OK, I paid the ten days, and don't worry; we will find something else," said Christian.

"OK, thank you. I don't have money at all, but I didn't want to say so in front of Hassan and Ramiz."

"You have nothing?"

"No. I left with nothing on me as Dad didn't want me to come."

"OK," said Christian thoughtfully. "We will find a solution. Maybe I can ask Hassan to speak with his aunt so you can stay permanently here; what do you think?"

"The room is horrible," said Laura.

"I am not allowed to go up and see, but they can do us a good price." He stared at her and then took a step back, holding her hands. "Don't worry; you will see me every day. You will only come here to sleep, that's all. Maybe you need time to get used to the idea. I won't push you. Just take your time, but don't forget we need to tell the nuns pretty soon, as there is a big demand for rooms here from Lebanese girls."

Laura had no choice. She didn't like Christian; she preferred Hassan, but what could she do but accept his offer?

"Sure," she said, hugging him. She knew she was manipulating him, but she felt no remorse. She hated waiting and not knowing, so she slid her hand up his back and kissed him.

When she came back that night, she saw a light shining from her room, so she knocked on the door.

"Enter," a voice said.

She opened the door and saw the back of her roommate who was getting dressed.

"Hi," said Laura in a very timid voice. "I am the new girl."

The girl turned. "Oh hi, nice to meet you. I am Amal. Are you a student?"

Laura felt uneasy. "Er…maybe, well I don't know. I mean I hope."

The girl looked at her puzzled. "Oh, don't worry; you will have plenty of time to decide. Why don't you come tonight to the television room in the communal area, and you can meet all the Lebanese girls here. We are a very close community here. Most of them are nice."

At 8:00 p.m. Laura appeared through the door, timid as usual, looking for Amal. Then she caught sight of a familiar face.

"Laura, is that you? It is me, Mary," said a tall striking girl, striding towards her in her unzipped dress. "What a surprise! What are you doing here? Come help me. I am trying a new dress that Penelope just bought for me."

Laura recognized Mary, her brother's nicest girlfriend.

"Mary, what are you doing here? I mean when did you move here? Walid never told me anything," she said, sitting on the chair.

"Ah, Walid! Your brother is a nightmare. Yeah when we split up, my mum sent me here. I've been living here for eight months. I didn't know you wanted to leave Lebanon. I had no idea. Go on talking to me while I change quickly."

"I couldn't stand living with Dad anymore; you know he is a difficult man."

"Yeah, maybe," said Mary, "but you are lucky to have a father; mine died when I was five."

"Yes, I'm sorry. I didn't mean to…"

"Don't worry. Anyway I have to go now," she said brightly.

"But you can't! How are you going to come back? They will shut the doors in thirty minutes."

"Don't worry; I sleep at my boyfriend's house, so I don't need to come back. See you tomorrow night? What about you? Any boyfriend?"

Laura felt a flash of annoyance and decided to ignore the second question. "Why not in the morning?"

Mary looked surprised by the question. "Ah, because I work at *la bourse de Paris*."

"What is that?" Laura asked, interested.

"It is *Marché a la Criee*, the financial market where people stand long hours and shout all day long." She laughed. "It's full of hot men—brokers and traders."

"Ah, and what do you do? You studied drama in Lebanon, so how did you find yourself working in finance?"

"You don't need to have any degree in finance; you only need to be fast."

"Fast?"

"Yes, speed is important—if you don't react quickly, you may lose money or you lose money for the bank or the broker you work for, and we are talking hundreds of thousands."

"Can I see it one day?"

"Sure you can, but don't wear that short skirt you've got on now; you look far too seductive," Mary drawled.

"Why not?" Laura asked.

"Because men will go crazy there; they'll stampede."

"And what do you exactly do there?"

"I work on the CAC forty futures—taking orders on the phone and communicating them to my broker through signs, but there are many other jobs like 'runners' where you have to give the ticket of the sale to the other counterpart once the deal is done."

"Anyway I will organize a visit for you, but now I have to rush."

"So happy to see you, Mary."

"Me too." She kissed Laura. "See you tomorrow," she said as she closed the door.

She seems so alive, Laura thought, so delighted with her world. I wish I could be like that. I must stay here in Paris, and I will do whatever I can, even if I have to make a pact with the devil. I will never go back to Lebanon.

Chapter 8

LAURA FOUND HERSELF a job as a sales assistant in a fashion shop on the Champs Elysees, aimed at a rich clientele. There she met a variety of people, and as the clients all came from wealthy backgrounds, she quickly attracted jealousy from her coworkers. She found she was persuasive with customers. She was pretty, and most of the men found her sexy. She developed from a shy, hesitant girl into a self-possessed woman confident of herself and her abilities. She worked there for nine months, but when the shop owner and manager discovered that she was stealing clothes, folding them very neatly in her lunch box, she couldn't defend herself except to say she needed to change her wardrobe and couldn't afford to because of her meagre salary. She was fired with no references, which made finding a new job more difficult.

Her father sent her money with letters full of insults, expressing his disappointment with her efforts. It was a struggle to read them, which prompted her to take any job available so she didn't have to go on living through this shame. Days passed; she suffered intense boredom, and her world seemed to have come to a halt. She needed action; immobility and silence were death to her. Her emotions died too, and she felt she had nothing to offer the world. She had wiped her memory slate clean and started joining protest marches, adopting every political cause as her own. In particular she marched to the Syrian embassy, protesting Syrian influence in Lebanon.

She had no main purpose in life, so she took any secondary role she found. People didn't want to listen to her, and anyway she felt she was miles apart from them in her ideas. She wasn't interested in their political games or their displays of money or their lies and pretentions. Nothing came from the soul; it was more like a boring rehearsal where she could foresee the ending. She needed more time and more experience to appear on that 'stage,' and she needed to know her audience and to be comfortable with them. She needed time, and she needed to be in love so she could find happiness. For now she was living through one deception after another, wasting love and energy. She immersed herself in love stories and books where miracles and fantasies could happen, where all kinds of colours and music beckoned her away from a world that had lost its colour and tone. She needed to change her world again but didn't know how; she no longer had the means. For her being in love was enough—wasn't it the basic thing that humans strove towards? Yet it was as if she'd asked for the impossible; nobody seemed to accept her. She knew she was not a normal person; she was a sort of halfway house where east met west and exchanged ideas and thoughts. She was a mixture of silk and incense, a rarity, a vivid collection, a mixture of worlds from Palestine, Egypt, Lebanon, and now Paris, and who knows where else. And she looked for Elias in every passerby, in every look and smell, hint or memory, trying to imagine where he was.

One day she found a job in a bookshop. The owner, Edward, was a pleasant, short man, enthusiastic about his collection and even more so about having a Lebanese as his coworker. She worked from nine until six; she found her clients boring, middle-aged intellectuals. It was there where she met Francois.

He was a clerk in a famous law firm. He was divorced with two children. He was quite a good-looking man in his forties, and he used to come and just sit and read after a hectic day with his demanding boss. He found tranquillity in the bookshop. Edward let him read his books, thinking he might use his services one day.

Laura started talking to him, using the usual polite phrases to direct him to books she thought he might be interested in. Eventually he began to open up to her and offered her a babysitting job after work, if she wanted to make extra money. She accepted and found herself in a small Parisian apartment, looking after two nice small children while Francois went to the movies alone. One night she put the kids in their respective beds and started reading a newspaper.

When he came back, she was asleep on the couch, and she woke up to see his hands reaching towards her face.

"Are you OK?" he asked.

Surprised, she answered, half asleep, "Huh…yes. The kids are OK. Lucy ate all her dinner, but Jean refused, so I had to cook something else. I hope you don't mind."

"Oh no, of course not, but you shouldn't have to cook, and he should eat what is on his plate."

"I'm sorry, but I didn't want him to go to sleep hungry."

"Never mind; do you want to go back home, or would you like to sleep here? If you want to sleep in my bed…I mean, I'll sleep here on the couch."

"All right; I'll sleep here."

"Good; great. Let me take my things, and then you can go to my room."

"Thank you," she muttered.

As soon as he appeared with a cushion and some bed sheets, she went to his room and prepared to go to bed. That's odd, she thought. I have a feeling we'll sleep together tonight. She took off her dress and put on one of his T-shirts that he had put neatly on the edge of the bed. When she looked towards the open door, he was looking at her. Oh gosh, he must have seen me naked, she thought, burning with embarrassment.

"Good night," he said.

"Good night."

Next morning she woke up to see him come into the room on his tiptoes, trying to grab a clean shirt.

"Did I wake you up, Laura?"

"No," she said, trying to sound awake. "But what's the time? Because I should go and get ready for work too."

"Why not stay here in my apartment for the day? I'll call Edward."

"No, it's fine. I really need to go and wash myself and put on my makeup. Do you want me to give your children breakfast?" she said as she rushed to the bathroom.

"They've already gone to school."

"Oh my God; what's the time?" she called out from behind the bathroom door.

"It's almost nine."

"I really should be going," she said, emerging from the bathroom, dressed for work.

"Laura? I put your money on the table. I counted the night as working hours."

"Thank you," she said as she grabbed the envelope, made her way out into the street, and rushed to the bus stop.

That day Francois didn't come to the bookshop as usual, but later he texted her, asking her if she could have dinner with him at home, after the children had gone to bed. She agreed although she found him as boring as hell.

She arrived around nine. He had cooked the only dish he knew, which was pasta with tomatoes, and added some salad on the side and a bottle of red wine.

"Are you comfortable?" he asked as they sat down.

"Yes, I'm fine; thank you."

"I hope you'll like my pasta."

"Normally I don't eat carbohydrates, but I will eat this."

"Oh, I'm so sorry. I didn't know. Next time I'll cook you a fish."

"How do you know Edward?" Laura asked.

"He's an old friend, and my office is next door to his bookshop."

"Do you like reading so much?"

"Yes, I do, but I don't have time with the kids, so I have to force myself to find the time to read every day."

After dinner she offered to help him with the dishes, but he refused inviting her to sit next to him on the sofa.

"You're very beautiful, Laura, but I'm too old for you. How old are you? In your early twenties I think."

"Yes, I am, and how old are you?"

"I'm forty-seven years old. I married very young but waited a long time before having kids. I wanted to enjoy being with my wife, but here we are...now I'm divorced."

"Why? You seem a nice guy to me."

"Well, I used to come home late from work; we would have a row, and then she would storm out and leave the house. One day she never came back; she left the kids with me and moved in with her tennis instructor. I hear they're getting married soon."

"I'm sorry to hear that, but you have two lovely kids."

"What about you? Any boyfriend or love? When did you leave Lebanon? Do you still have any family there?"

Laura started to relax. She allowed her head to loll back and then closed her eyes. She was exhausted; she didn't care about his pathetic life. She felt sorry for him but could offer him nothing. She didn't like his questions; he wanted to open the small window onto her life, but she felt uncomfortable about letting him into her life. He was being too intrusive, and besides he wasn't much younger than her father.

"Oh," he said. "I sense here a lost love."

He seemed to wake her up, and she fumbled in her pocket for a tissue and blew her nose.

"Sorry…um…I left Lebanon two years ago, and yes, my family is there."

"I see; so you live alone here?"

"Why are you asking me?"

"I just like you and would love to hang out with you if you would like me to."

She looked into his eyes and lied. "Of course I do."

"Really?" He looked at her with a big smile and kissed her. He had a clean-shaven face and a swarthy complexion, not unpleasant, but she shivered involuntarily.

"I want to make love to you; it's been so long," he muttered.

This last detail horrified her and made her uncomfortable. Why would she care about this guy and his needs? Yet she followed him to the bedroom, and he was a kind and attentive lover. Afterwards he took a long drag on his cigarette, and with a sigh he looked at her.

"You are fantastic; do you know that?"

"Thank you," she answered.

"Did you enjoy it as much as I did?"

"Yes," she lied again.

"Spend the night with me here then."

"No; I really have to go now as last time I was a mess."

"OK then," he held her hand. "When will I see you next?"

"I'll call you," she said. She got dressed and hurried out of the house and then hailed a taxi and went back to her room.

→═◎ ◎═←

Once in her room, she felt submerged in a huge sadness. She watched her goldfish, Tatiana, imprisoned in her tank, swimming around all day long with nowhere else to go. Tatiana depended on her for food and clean water. Her life was like Tatiana's, stuck in a bowl all day, not knowing what to do.

They saw each other several times after that. He was always nice to her and generous. But she couldn't see a future or a life with him. So she decided it should stop. She couldn't take him, with his loneliness and silent dinners with no jokes and no spirit. You could only hear the clock on the wall. He was as dusty as his files. She imagined his office filled with hundreds of files piled up high on a table, waiting for his signature, and then his pathetic routine, finishing at five and heading towards the library, just to read another boring book that Edward had selected for him so he could help him out one day. She wanted to be part of the world, not this sad story; she definitely needed to leave him now before he got more attached.

One morning she headed to work as usual when she received a message from Francois, wishing her a beautiful day. She ignored it; then when she saw him as usual at five, she had already asked permission from Edward to leave on time. She was preparing her bag when Francois arrived. He seemed to be out of breath and must have run to see her.

"Hi," he said, with beads of sweat on his forehead. "Can you come with me to the movies tonight? I arranged for another babysitter to come."

She felt uncomfortable and gazed at the floor. After a moment she straightened up.

"No, and I don't want to be your girlfriend. I'm in love with someone else. I mean I...have a boyfriend," she said in a hesitant voice.

"Oh really! So where is he? This mysterious boyfriend."

His mocking tone irritated her. "He's been travelling, but he's coming back today," she said defiantly.

"So if you are in love with him, why did you have sex with me?"

"I don't know. Not sure why. I am sorry," she said, flicking her hair back and casting her eyes on the bookshelf.

He nodded and wiped his sweaty palm down his trouser leg. "Hmm, OK, no problem. Enjoy and have fun."

She took her bag and left in a hurry. Once outside she breathed fresh air and felt relieved. Francois leaned against the wall, his head tilted up, his eyes blinking. He took the plastic water bottle from the pocket of his coat and spilled it on his hair. He had a hollow look in his eyes and then brushed his hair with his hand as he walked away slowly.

--⇥≡◉ ◉≡⇤--

Laura propped her bicycle up and chained it to the railings of the Luxembourg Gardens. She looked at her watch to make sure she'd arrived ten minutes early for her appointment to meet her friend Mary when suddenly she heard her voice and turned to find Mary standing there.

"Hey, so happy to see you; it's been so long," Mary said.

"Hello, I missed you too. I was busy working at the bookshop two doors down from here, but I quit, so I have more time."

"So you're looking for a job?"

"Yes, I am. If you hear of something, please tell me."

"OK. I'll see if there is anything available in the bourse where I work. They are looking for people. I'll ask my boyfriend, Rami, tomorrow."

"That would be great as I have to pay my room rent. The nuns gave me another month, but I really need to pay them, otherwise they'll throw me out."

"They won't; they're nuns."

"They will, believe me, because they're building new accommodation, and they need the money."

"Anyway how is everything with you? Did you hear anything from Elias?"

"No, I'm trying to track him down. I asked my mother to call his mother, but she refused."

"Why did she refuse?" asked Mary.

"Because they don't know each other well, and then, of course my mother doesn't like him."

"But she never met him, right?"

"Yes, but I told her about him. I don't know; she never liked the boys I knew anyway."

"So what are you going to do then?"

"I don't know."

"Let's call her now. Give me the number."

"Now? Tell her that you are a good friend of Elias."

"OK, come on, there's a public phone booth; let's try to call her."

Mary dialled the number; then after a while she spoke.

"Hello, Tante, it's me Mary. I'm a good friend of Elias, and I need to speak with him please."

Laura was jumping around, giggling like a young girl.

"Oh, I'm really sorry to hear that," Mary seemed sad. "OK, so he didn't call you since, I see…oh my God. OK. No worries. Sorry for bothering you. Good-bye."

Mary hung up the phone and looked at Laura. She stubbed out her cigarette and lit up another one. "Your Elias had two deaths in his family lately—his uncle and his father. He left the farm, and she doesn't know his whereabouts as he stopped calling her since his uncle was shot dead," she told Laura.

"Shot dead? That's dreadful! So is he still in Brazil?"

"Don't know. The poor lady was almost in tears."

"I see."

She felt a sudden rush of panic at this news and held her breath. Now that he was gone into the wild she might never see him again.

"He's gone," she said.

Mary pressed her finger to Laura's lips, which stopped her panic abruptly.

"Don't be so negative; you never know. If you're meant to be together, then you will be."

Laura rolled her eyes. "You're right. I always believed everything you told me," she said, looking her friend up and down, appraising her.

"Now come on," Mary said. "Let's go and get a bite to eat."

⇥ ◉ ◈⇤

A month later Laura was lying on her bed, looking at the ceiling, when the phone rang. It was Mary on the phone, asking Laura if she'd be interested in working with her and a group of Lebanese at the Bourse de Paris.

The next day Laura met with Toni, the recruiter, a fat Lebanese guy. He took her around and showed her the *Marche a la Crieé*. She was impressed but at the same time terrified. The place was a huge, open trading floor, and the atmosphere was male dominant. Speed was essential, and if she was wrong, it could be costly to her employer and to her.

Toni was a very imposing guy in his midthirties. He'd been brought up in Scotland and didn't seem Lebanese, with his red hair and fair skin. He was hugely respected by his coworkers. After showing her the market, he took her to collect her vest, which was an orange colour. All the bankers and brokers had their own vests with different colours and insignia according to what they did. Her job was on the lower scale, and yet it was a very important role as she would keep track of the trading positions. Once inside she panicked, as she was terrible at maths, and the stress was huge. She ran to Toni and told him that she'd thought about it but that she wouldn't be able to do the job. He grabbed her hand and took her out to look through a huge glass wall where he could see the trading on the floor.

He shouted at her, "Look around you."

"OK. I'm looking," she said.

"No, look more," he shouted. "If they can do it, then so can you! They're not more intelligent than you."

Laura went back inside the bourse and found some confidence. She never feared working there again. Days passed by, and as her salary increased, she started looking around to rent an apartment in the suburbs of Paris on the advice of the Lebanese friends she made while working there. She met some nice men at work, and she dated some of them while others she viewed with suspicion.

One of them attracted her attention particularly, and she fell in love, quickly as usual. Olivier reminded her of a neighbour; he was handsome and very young with a beautiful racing car. They met several times and made love, but he told her he was in love with his best friend's girlfriend. One day he suggested they go out in his sports car for a drive in the country. He waited for her outside her apartment. She came out of her front door and jumped into the passenger seat. She leaned back in the seat and just gazed at the sky and the clouds as the car sped down the road.

"There's something fascinating about going on the road alone," Olivier said as he accelerated. "You're faced with your demons and fears in this static land-scape; it reminds me of a painting."

"It's not a painting," Laura protested. "It's moving and changing all the time." Then she added, "It's big monuments that make me feel so small."

"Why do you measure yourself to such big reference points?" Olivier asked.

She crossed her legs and pulled up her skirt in an attempt to catch his at-tention, but his mind was elsewhere. He seemed distracted. He reached in his pocket, took out a cigarette, and offered her one.

"No, thank you. I don't smoke or drink, but you go ahead," she said, and then she gently caressed his face; she was entranced by him.

He looked at her. "What do you do then?"

"I eat chocolate," she laughed.

He pulled the car into a nice park and turned towards her. "Do you want to walk a bit?"

"Yes, sure," she said. They went towards a secluded spot under a tree and sat together in silence. She hoped he would grab her and kiss her, but he didn't. Laura felt a sickening feeling of loneliness. She thought, Please God, don't let it happen again. I want this boy above everything; please do something. He turned towards her and said, "We definitely have nothing to say to each other."

She was taken aback by his unusual aggressive tone. "I am sure it's coming from you, as you're always thinking about this girl."

"Which girl?" He swivelled round to face her and smiled; then his eyes left her.

"Joe's girlfriend."

"No, I told you we stopped a long time ago. I told her I couldn't go on like that."

"So why are you so distracted and strange today?"

"No, I'm not. I'm just at a contemplative stage in my life."

"And of course I have no place in this stage?"

"Laura, I like you a lot; you're a nice girl, but I need to find someone else. I prefer to tell you than to keep on seeing you and cheat on you."

"Oh no! Why did you bring me here to tell me this?" she cried, and then got up and dusted herself, her eyes beginning to mist with tears behind her sunglasses.

"Look, I thought it is better to tell you here rather than over the phone."

"Really? Well, very much appreciated—thank you very much!"

"I should take you home now," he said.

"Yes, I suppose you should," Laura said absently. She was still trying to catch and appreciate the sensation of being next to him. She knew that after this, she would never be with him again.

"By the way, it's the girl you have been working with. You like her a lot; this is why you are leaving me to be with her?" she asked.

"Who? Janine? Why do you say that?" he asked.

"Because you're always together."

"We work together—no more, no less."

He pulled out his keys and headed towards the car. His shoulders looked narrow in his oversized leather jacket. She was devastated; probably Francois had felt the same. She had been cruel to him; now someone else was cruel to her. As they drove back, he seemed relieved and peaceful, but for her it was a cruel silence. It was the worst of all tortures. Words could be hurtful, but silence was even worse. A contemptuous look could hurt more than no look at all. She felt a growing void within her.

They arrived back at her apartment, and she got out of the car without saying good-bye. She ran up the stairs, taking the steps two at a time, then opened her door, and slammed it shut behind and started crying. She felt pain going through her head. So cruel! How could someone be so cruel and reject her so brutally?

They had only been dating for the last three weeks, and he obviously didn't care for her. A month after they split up, he announced his engagement to Janine.

She tried to forget him as much as she could but it was difficult. She went to every church and prayed to God to bring him back to her, but nothing happened. She started calling him just to hear his voice, but one day he faced her and told her to stop, so she lied and said it was Mary who'd been calling; then she ran to see Mary and told her.

"What? What did you tell him? Are you out of your mind?" Mary shouted.

"I know. I'm sorry…just didn't know what to say."

"Why involve me in your stories? Find yourself someone else to put the blame on. I don't want to talk to you anymore. I'm done with you," said Mary as she walked away carelessly, glancing once over her shoulder.

"I'm sorry," Laura shouted, but it was too late; she knew now that she had lost her best friend and the boy she loved.

Scared of being alone with her dark thoughts, Laura finally returned Francois's calls. He invited her 'as a friend' to his favourite local brasserie. She accepted the invitation. Laura put on a tight crimson dress and pulled her hair back in a ponytail. To him she was like a fresh breeze on a midsummer day. Her beauty and her tight breasts fascinated Francois.

"We were very intimate very briefly," he said once they sat down and started to talk.

"Yes, for a short time," she agreed.

"Well, it felt good…to me. But yes, I'm sorry; you were scared, Laura."

"A bit, maybe; is that bad?"

"No, I respect your feelings."

"Ah…but—"

"Sorry, I interrupted you," he said.

"Don't worry."

"I do worry."

"Why? You don't need to," she said.

"Because you'll disappear again."

"Oh…don't say that. I didn't abandon you. I was just taken aback. It was too much too quickly."

"In a way you did. But I'm still your friend," Francois said.

"True. Did you feel abandoned?"

"Yes."

"I thought that by living twelve years of civil war, God would spare me other people's wickedness."

"Life doesn't work like that, Laura."

"I know; life doesn't owe us anything. It's not a land of wishes."

"Stay positive, Laura."

"I'm trying."

"You have every reason to."

"But it's hard. I'm not sure of anything, let alone my existence and conscience. I know I exist because of the food I need to eat and the air I need to breath, but I don't have proof of anything, and it's so sad."

There was silence at the table. Then after some time, Francois said, "The silence means I am thinking about what you are saying."

"I know. Yesterday I sat on a bench in the park, looking at boats going up and down the river," Laura said, gazing at him.

"I can't tell you how to take the sadness out of your life, Laura, but I can tell you that you need to try and focus on the good things."

"I'm trying, but it's hard," she said. "Sometimes I wonder if I have ever loved or existed in another person's life."

"Well, in a pure Cartesian world, you might not be wrong. But to be you, you need to *be* socially…so we have to learn to accept that we are also made up of a sequence of social events. We exist as temporal social beings, as without social engagement we would just go crazy."

"What to do then?"

"That's why we develop prejudice as a self-defence mechanism. I don't have the solution, but reading contemporary history helped me a lot with this."

"So actually we exist only in relation to other people?"

"Well, maybe you could say we exist as individual experiences of life."

"I see."

"Only if you allow that to define you, Laura."

"What about the outcasts or people in the asylum? Or the rejected?"

"Well, first be at peace with yourself; then tend to others. That's why in the safety procedures before any takeoff, they always tell you in case of emergency landing to put your seat belt first and then do it for your child. It sounds cruel," he added, "but it makes good sense."

"Do you take care of yourself?" she looked at him.

"I don't know…I try."

"I'm just trying to. It's not easy, but I should, and you should too."

"No, I know," he said. "But when you see yourself going down, make yourself change and go up."

"Like the movie *Gone with the Wind*. Scarlett O'Hara says 'Tomorrow is another day.'"

"I didn't see that," he said.

"You should; it's the most beautiful love story ever."

"It's a chick flick, I guess," he smiled.

"No, not really."

"Are there any guns, or is it all sex and kisses?"

"No, there's war. It's set during the American Civil War."

"I see. Anyway how is your new job? You seemed very excited about it."

"Yes, I'm very happy. I moved, and I have my own small flat."

"So maybe you can invite me for dinner one day. As a friend," he laughed. Then he looked at her. "Laura, we need to reach an agreement. We should stay friends and be fond of each other but not obsessed."

"Yes, I agree," she said. "It was great to see you, but I should be going now."

"You're always rushing to leave me; wait a bit." He held her arm as she was preparing to take her bag.

"Are you in love, Laura?"

"No," she lied. "Why are you asking me this?"

"So the boyfriend story was a lie, I was sure. Anyway there is no reason to my question, but you will find someone when you least expect it; it's always like that…"

"I need to find someone who is better than me. I need to learn and be challenged."

"OK. All right, darling, but it's not a competition."

"No, you're right, but I do need someone who's educated at least as much as my dad, who speaks several languages."

"But why? Maybe you'll find someone who is formally ignorant but carries the wisdom of life? What do you want, Laura? A diamond in a mountain of crystal? It'll be harder to find—not impossible, but harder, yes."

"That's true," she said and kissed him on the cheek and left the restaurant.

Months passed, and Laura found she didn't want to be with anyone. Lots of boys asked her out, but she found them all dull. Then one of them, from the south of France, insisted a bit more, and he caught her attention. He worked with her but as a market maker for a French bank. He took her out to dinner and couldn't take his eyes off her. Holding her hand and squeezing it gently, he said, "You are very beautiful." She looked pained as he said, "I never dreamed that someone like you would ever look at me."

He was a tall man, well built with grey hair, although young, and dark-green eyes. His name was Louis. He marvelled at her sweeping eyelashes, her rosy cheeks, and lips, and then he leaned over and kissed her gently.

He was different from the others, very romantic, but a bit peculiar. After nine months she decided to marry him, not knowing anything about the real implications of marriage.

Louis Bauvier had severed all ties with his family for years especially with his father, John, who had written volumes of diaries on his own children, grandchildren, and even his wife.

Louis and Laura married in a lavish wedding ceremony in a quiet haven in Nice on August 5, 1989, five years after Laura's arrival in Paris. There were more than a hundred and fifty guests at the wedding party from all over the world, and Laura's parents came from Lebanon. The wedding day was hot, and the guests enjoyed three days of celebrations.

Soon after it became obvious that Louis and Laura were very different. Louis was a quiet man, didn't much like people, and distrusted family in general; he became jealous of Laura's relationship with her mother.

"Are you all right? You spoke to your mother again today, I guess?" he asked, perched next to her on the sofa.

"And?" her voice trailed off.

"Nothing; it is just an observation. I hope you don't tell her everything about us. I am very private, and you know that. I understand she is your mother, but I don't particularly like her." He grinned and licked his lips with a cocky smile.

"Why is that? You are just an obnoxious asshole." Then she left the room.

"I was expressing my opinion. By the way all these calls to Beirut cost a fortune," he shouted sarcastically.

Little by little Laura became lonely. She kept any opinions to herself. The atmosphere inside the house became stuffy; the walls between her and Louis became higher and thicker. She isolated herself from her friends and from Louis's parents and siblings. Louis tried hard to cope with Laura's constant rejection to have sex with him. One afternoon he grabbed her hand, pulled her closely to him, and then made love to her.

⸱⟶ ⟵⸱

When she discovered she was pregnant, Laura went to see her doctor, sobbing.

"What on earth is happening, Laura?" her doctor asked.

"I can't have this baby. I am in a panic of impending motherhood. What happens if I fail this baby? I don't think I'm ready."

The doctor stared at her slack-jawed. "You may be afraid, but don't worry; everything is going to be OK. Just relax. I'm sure you will be a great mother. Anyway if you continue feeling that way, I really advise you to see a therapist."

Louis was ecstatic. He always wanted a girl. However, it was a very difficult pregnancy, and Laura needed to lie down for the last six months to prevent the contractions and keep the baby.

Nine months later her daughter, Leila, arrived—a very sweet blond girl. Laura loved her beyond anything; she wanted to offer her the best and became fiercely protective of her. Louis would awake two to three times a night just to feed her.

Laura could not let her baby go from her arms. Only by constantly hugging her did she feel safe. She showered Leila with toys and clothes, but things started to deteriorate between her and Louis. She felt she was becoming a closed book with no chapters or headings. She felt she was writing someone else's story and had moved from an active role in her personal life to a spectator of a life she no longer knew how to live.

⤙⬤ ⬤⤚

Laura lived a lie, an inauthentic existence, during her marriage. She tried to convince herself that this was her role in life to be a mother and a wife, following the sermons of her father. One day she was sitting cross-legged looking out of the window of her apartment at a couple making love in an apartment in front of her. Drifting off in her mind, she imagined herself as this girl. She needed so much to be touched. Drawing her knees to her chest, she felt so envious. She had only felt this for a short period in Lebanon. She tried to find these moments, but she seemed to have lost them forever. She shook her head, and the tears started flowing. "What have I done with my life?" she kept repeating, rocking back and forth on her chair. She never loved Louis—that was the truth, the bleak reality, the big lie. How could someone lie to herself? All this social and religious guilt—she wished she could shout and tell the truth. Her mother kept on telling her, "Never mind; you need him," but it was such a stupid thing to say. How about "Never mind I need myself first; I need myself to be sane, and then I will think of him." How come everything I did so far is wrong, she thought. She did not want to end up unhappy like her mother, but the truth was that she was already unhappy. She could not blend in here; it was a different culture, and the sad thing was that Louis was unaware of all this. He barely knew her, and they had their daughter so quickly and unexpectedly. She turned away slowly when she heard Louis arriving home.

"Hi, darling, how was your day?"

She wiped her tears and pretended to speak normally. "Yeah, I'm fine; we just came back from the park. How was your day?"

"Oh, as usual."

She couldn't deal with this expression anymore. "As usual"—what does he mean by that? How could a whole life be "as usual"? What is usual to begin with? She folded her hands behind her head.

"You're in a bad mood; I can see that," he said.

She looked at him nervously. "You just arrived home, and you want to pick a fight?"

"No, I'm not actually; I was in a good mood," he said.

She pointed out of the window. "Look, that couple is making love."

"And?"

"They look happy."

"You always envied other people's lives."

"That's a feeble excuse," she said.

"Excuse for what?"

"Nothing; don't worry," she said and went to the kitchen. "What do you want to eat?"

"Whatever you want."

"No, what do you desire?"

"Oh, nothing particular—as you wish."

Things became tense. She didn't know exactly when, but there is a moment suspended in time when things are good and then they are not. This moment is not defined in time, but it exists, and once we are on the other side of this time, things can never go back. She always thought she deserved better in life, but in order to achieve it, you should not reveal your true feelings. She always thought that once her dad died, she would go to his room and talk to him and finally tell him what she thought of him. How could she be genuine? Being genuine for her was to walk away alone. She did it once in her life, and now she regretted it.

Once Louis came to her room. "You know, Laura, I don't think you love me."

"Why? What made you say that? Of course I love you."

"At least on your deathbed, you can say that you were once loved, but I can't say this about myself," he said sadly.

"Why do you say that?"

"I don't know. I can see it in your eyes, or actually I can see how you love our daughter, and this has nothing to do with how you feel towards me."

"Don't be silly; it is the same love but a different way of expressing it," Laura remonstrated.

He stammered apologies and walked away. He knew he was right and was convinced that Laura didn't love him. He just didn't know how to get her back. He loved her immensely, and yet he resented her lack of compassion. He was ready to fight to keep the family united, but he wasn't sure how far he was ready to compromise. Laura was an inherently unhappy person. He recognized it as she reminded him of himself and the sad time of his childhood—when he lost his first love, he became drunk for two years, not thinking straight and losing himself in the arms of women he disliked. He drowned his soul in a sea of despair and then packed his stuff and left the family. Laura was a new beginning, and he vowed to keep her at any price even if bits of himself were falling apart.

Laura felt terrible; her hands were tied up in a painful iron grip—it was like a performance that was imposed with an automatic answer to a very common question. How could she say "Of course not, let us break now; please give me my freedom so I can leave"? She was not brought up to be mean but to be compassionate, and not blunt. She fell to her knees and started sobbing. "It's not his fault; it's mine. It's so cruel that he should pay for it." He was not up to her expectations; she needed a strong man who would pin her to the wall and undress her and make love to her, not Louis asking her opinion on everything.

"You need a stronger man," he said once, and his face sagged. "I'm too weak for you."

"What makes you say that?"

"Maybe the next one will be luckier than me. I don't understand you, Laura."

"You don't need to. Just love me properly, stop drinking and moaning, and let's see a doctor together to deal with your sexual problem."

"It's always me who is to blame. You're spotless."

"OK. Let's do nothing then."

"Always white or black with you."

Laura rubbed her throat as she heard him take the bins outside and, as he did every night, go for a walk. The hot slow breeze carried with it memories of Beirut. She missed her hometown a lot. She missed every moment of it. One thing she was sure of was that she was very unhappy and nothing could change that. Then she broke into loud sobs.

Chapter 9

THE ATMOSPHERE IN the house was dreadful with little to say and lots to shout about. All her dreams were shattered; she could not believe that after dreaming of all these love stories, her life was so plain and meaningless. She enjoyed her life as a mother, but she dreaded it as a wife and a woman. There was no exit. She started to think about going out with other men, and her thoughts started to find refuge in other men's arms, dreaming of a love that could uproot her and throw her like seeds in the wind.

There was a part of her that wished that she could love him in the way that he did love her, but her heart had been broken irreparably many times before. Louis started drinking heavily and staying late after work in local bars. It was the same story when she called him to know where he was; he would put the phone down after picking up and promising to go home instantly. He struggled with a sexual problem, and she tried to convince him to see someone about this, but he wouldn't listen. For his part he was fine—she was the frigid one. He even went as far as to suggest her father must have raped her when she was young. Sex was always a very sad experience where he would come and she would be crying, looking at the ceiling, all night long. He would then promise her that next time it would be better.

Financially they struggled, as he was not paid as well as his colleagues. There was always a discrepancy between his wage and that of other people he worked with. Yet he never had the courage to face his boss and ask for compensation and fair treatment. Instead he would turn to her and fly into a rage and tell her to go back to work if she wasn't happy. Louis always knew that it was only a matter of time with Laura as he was convinced that she didn't love him. He knew that deep down she could never forget her first childhood friend.

He had aged in a rugged way, and his hair turned even greyer. He became very lazy and didn't want to go to work. He lost all ambition, and Laura struggled with that as it reminded her of her father. She gradually lost the energy to challenge him or answer him back. For the last six months, the situation was difficult but something in her grew resolute and focused. She realized she needed to do something about her life. She couldn't bear the death of love, so she just stopped loving him. He was too weak, and she couldn't handle it. She needed a warrior to protect her and her daughter. She had to challenge reality with all its inevitability.

One day she faced him after he came from work. "I am leaving you," she said.

"Bitch, after what I've done for you? But you're not taking my daughter," he scowled. He was clearly taken by surprise and hadn't expected her to announce a separation.

"Your answer is so typical. Surprise me for once," she shouted.

"What do you want me to tell you? Give me another chance!"

"No, I can't. We've run out of chances."

He looked confused; he sat cross-legged on the bed while she was perched on the dark oak chair by the window.

"There are several issues, and I don't see us reaching an agreement," she said.

He raised his eyebrows. "I know."

"I've been thinking lately how best to help you; maybe you need to see a therapist?" she suggested.

"I have a very stressful job, and your demands are huge. I am trying to deliver, but it's too hard."

"Perhaps, but I can't deal with it. Louis, I'm leaving you."

"Where will you go?" His eyes widened; then his features rearranged themselves into a martyr-like expression. "You're destroying the family."

"Am I? Am I to blame now? You never face your responsibilities; it's always others people's fault," she shouted back. Then tears started to fall from her eyes.

"Your parents hate me for no good reason. Oh, maybe it's because they're racist, and I'm not French."

"They're idiots, and you know that. Why does it matter now?"

"Because there's no family support. I'm exhausted, and you need a mother, not a wife."

"We can't go on like this," he said. "So where are you going? You're not answering my question, and of course you must have found another man."

"I'll live with Mary for a bit," she said. "And then I'll see if I can move and leave the country."

He sat up a little straighter and paused. "Oh, I see; so you figured out everything with that bitch Mary."

"You always hated everyone; all my friends and basically everybody around us. Stop being sarcastic all the time."

He stood up and nodded and then paused awkwardly. "I'm going out."

He put on his jacket and pulled up his collar. Laura watched him, a look of hopelessness on her face. He stopped, turned round, and waited. "Good luck," he said. Then he left. No further words were exchanged, but they both knew it was the end. Louis cried while walking. That's it, he thought. You fucked it up again.

Then he sat on the edge of a small wall, smoking nervously; the light rain didn't bother him. He took his phone from his pocket, called his best friend Marco, and headed to the café nearby for the usual drink.

That was it, Laura thought. Almost six years of marriage and that's all? Maybe she wanted him to stop her and beg her, but he did not; that was Louis. She was astonished how people could just walk away as if nothing happened without a proper good-bye. She packed her things and left with her daughter to go and live with Mary.

⋆⟶⊙ ⊙⟵⋆

Mary opened the door, surprised. "Is everything OK?" she inquired anxiously.

"Everything is fine now," Laura answered.

"You're not surprised, are you?" She looked at Mary. "You knew it would happen."

"Yes," replied Mary. "I knew you were miserable for too long. I'm not blind even if I don't live with you guys. It wasn't too hard to figure out. I always had my doubts."

"Yeah," replied Laura. "There's no point going back now. Thank you for accepting us. We won't be staying long; I promise."

Laura continued jobless as she had left her work as soon she'd married Louis and became a mother. She filed for divorce, and in the meantime her husband went into heavy depression followed by several panic attacks. This prompted his human-resources department to ask him to take some time off work. The divorce came through, and her father refused to speak to her ever since she'd told him her decision on the phone. For him marriage was forever; a woman should not divorce. "What God united nobody can disunite," he used to shout.

Louis finally gave her his blessing and started dating his first cousin. Laura felt disappointed and suspected he had been having an affair during their marriage, as later Louis confided in her that he had been in contact with her all the time by e-mail. Losing Laura was a heavy blow on Louis; he suddenly realized that although their marriage suffered considerably, he had beautiful memories with her. Laura was a tortured soul yet very lively. His life was never the same.

Chapter 10

SWEATING UNDER THE fierce heat, Elias peeled off his T-shirt and put on a new one from the bag he had left on the wood piled up outside the shed and then waved wildly to Ricardo.

"Let's go, amigo; too hot today!"

Inside the bar slouched on a bar stool, he scowled as he described his hectic day to the local bartender. Then he turned towards Ricardo.

"Shall we eat? I know you must be starving."

"Yes, no problem; they do the best tapas in town here."

"Let's share some."

"Yeah, cool."

Elias played with his food and felt too exhausted even to eat.

"How are things with your uncle?"

"I don't know. I'm thinking about giving up this tough life and leaving this shitty place. I'm so tired—can't take it anymore."

"Lucky you; I don't have a choice. I have five kids to feed. I don't know why you don't go back to Lebanon; you must have family there," Ricardo responded, his mouth half full.

"Nah, I don't want that. It's too late to turn back now. We're still a country at war." He bit into his taco and moaned, "That's delicious!"

"I told you! Best place in town."

"What do you think about my uncle's girlfriend?"

"Who?"

"The blond one? Sally? Oh yes, she's been coming here for a long time. She doesn't interfere in his affairs at all. I think there was a big drama in her life. I think she lost a child, poor woman."

"Some people bury the past, but that doesn't give you a chance to look back at it. I think this woman buried it forever. Some cultures in Africa create an old man out of straw and dress him very poorly and then they bury him, thinking they bury their poverty and bad luck with it," Elias replied.

Ricardo continued, "I don't know if you heard, but your uncle is in deep trouble with the local governor over the shooting of a trespasser on his land. This chap was his nephew. Giuseppe thinks he can settle it with few reals, but the mother is asking for revenge, and you know these people are farmers; they have nothing. Your uncle is the *rico* of the *aldeia*, and they want a lot more."

"I know you mentioned it to me last time but very briefly. I didn't know it was so serious, but the guy was a thief, wasn't he?" Elias asked.

"His mother says no and that he happened to be there by mistake. Your uncle was drunk that day, so he shot him."

"So why was he there then? The farm is so big; he must have known it was private property...I don't know what to think, but it's hard to discuss anything with him or even to express an opinion."

"True but we should do something. The pressure is mounting from the family, and the local governor has to please them as the election is soon, and he may lose his seat to his rival."

"Like Pontius Pilate with Jesus!" said Elias. "Where my uncle would be sacrificed for political ambition."

"A strange comparison," Ricardo said. "You forget that Jesus didn't kill anybody."

"True. Anyway thanks for the food. I'll get the bill. I want to go home."

Elias felt the need to call Sally. He suddenly missed her voice and her wise words. As he stood up, he saw a movement in his peripheral vision. Wide eyed, he stared at the governor approaching him very slowly. He felt a shiver creep down his neck and turned his face away.

"You are Giuseppe's nephew if I am not mistaken."

"Yes, I guess I am," he replied and shook his hand.

"Are you thirsty for another beer?"

"Oh, I was about to go."

"I will only stay for few minutes, and I won't take much of your time. Let me get the bill."

Elias hesitated and then sat down grimacing. Ricardo excused himself.

"Elias, sorry, I have to go back to my wife, otherwise she'll worry. See you tomorrow."

They sat at the corner of the restaurant. A Coca-Cola sign hanging above the governor's head distracted Elias from the serious conversation.

"Look, we are in big trouble here," said the governor. "You must have heard. You know I like your uncle, and he did a lot of good things to this village, donated money to our school and hospital, but this doesn't excuse him from executing a twenty-three-year-old boy in cold blood on the basis that he trespassed on his land. He also has a real problem with alcohol, and we have to sort out the mess."

Elias dropped his chin for a moment and then stared back at the governor with an odd look on his face.

"He didn't execute the guy in cold blood. I am sure Giuseppe had his reasons. People were trying to steal from his land, and he is the only one who defends it. What do you mean by sorting things out? What do you propose?"

"I don't know, but we can settle this with money."

"How much?"

"We are talking a million or so."

"A million? But I know Giuseppe doesn't have that much."

"Then he should sell the farm and move somewhere else."

"The farm is his life," Elias said, jumping to his feet.

"A life for a life," the governor sighed. "I need you to work with me, not against me."

"This is my uncle, my blood. I can't be with you against family."

The governor twisted slightly to face Elias. "So you are against me," he said in a menacing voice.

Elias pursed his lips. "Then, yes, I am against you," he said and stormed out.

⇥◉ ◉⇤

The next day Elias looked at the sofa where his uncle sat sipping his whisky with a cigar on his lips and a haze of smoke swirling above his head. He wore a light-blue shirt pulling tight over his generous belly. The room smelled mouldy and rusty; cheap candles stuck out from candelabras on the chimneypiece. Elias settled in the couch facing him.

"I haven't seen so much looting in the farm since I first settled here," Giuseppe said, griming around his cigar; "Since you arrived here, you've handled your stint admirably, Elias."

The candlelight flickered, showing Giuseppe's lips expelling a deep even breath; he looked exhausted.

Elias ignored his uncle's words and just asked him, "Hey, how was your day?"

Giuseppe peered at him; he was busy counting the missing sheep. "Where did you go? I waited to have dinner with you! You could have told me you were going to town."

Elias rubbed his chin. "Yeah, sorry, I went to Margarita's with Ricardo. It was freaking hot this afternoon, so I went for a cold beer and some handmade tortillas."

"Yes, I use to go there. I knew the owner. A pretty hardworking girl. Since she sold it, I don't go there anymore. Now I like staying home with my whisky and a cigar." He scratched his head and grinned. "Do you want to go fishing tomorrow, Elias, like the old days?"

"Sure!" Elias replied nonchalantly. "We haven't done that for ages. Sounds great."

"OK. I'll tell Eduardo to prepare everything for us. We have to go early; not like last time…" he said, heaving himself up from the sofa. "OK. So I'm going to my bed now."

Elias stayed, watching TV, flicking from one channel to another. The wax spilled over the candelabras, hardening as it did, creating weird shapes. He gazed at them for a long time; then he took the phone and pressed on Sally's number. After a while a warm voice answered.

"*Bon dia.*"

"Hello, it's me."

"Hello, Elias! It's been soooo long. How are you? How are things?"

"I'm fine; just got back from a nice meal. Thought I'd give you a shout."

"Oh, that's nice. Where did you go?"

"Margarita's."

"Oh, the local tapas? I've never been, but I heard from Giuseppe that it's good. Apart from that how is work? I still have to arrange with your uncle a suitable weekend when you can both come and relax in my garden."

"Well, definitely not tomorrow; we're going fishing on the lake," he said with a tired grin.

"Fishing? You're kidding me, right? Last time I went with him, we didn't catch one fish. All he wanted to do was drink and gaze at the lake."

"Then that will make two of us! I don't have the patience for that kind of thing either by the way." Elias paused for a moment before continuing, "I am just a bit concerned. I saw the governor today at Margarita's. He was very menacing regarding the shooting. I'm worried about Giuseppe's safety. Do you think he is safe?"

"Depends. What do you mean by 'safe'?"

"I don't know. I have a bad feeling about the whole thing."

"Don't worry; your uncle is a tough cookie. I'm sure they'll settle; I am fairly certain. It is only now a question of how much, and it took a year to reach this solution!"

"Really? What was the situation before?"

"Well, they wanted to put him in a prison for ten years."

"I didn't know that. OK, I feel a bit more relaxed. I don't want to sound ridiculous, but I don't want to stay away from you."

That amused her, but she didn't want to show her excitement.

"Me neither, but you decided that; do you remember?"

There was a silence when Elias felt stunned by her graciousness. He took a deep long breath and then dried the sweat on his scalp. The garden view in front of him suddenly looked bare. He was happy it was wintertime; he huddled under the thick sofa cover that the maid had arranged carefully.

"It's simply that my mind is somewhere else…I just don't want to leave until I…"

"Don't say anything; just breathe, Elias. I just want to hear your breath."

The truth was that he hadn't contacted her regarding Giuseppe though that was part of it, but he had missed her. He strained his eyes into the dark. "When will I see you?"

"Let me organize something with him. I will call him tomorrow; I promise. Goodnight; sleep well, and don't worry."

Elias put the phone down. He felt a huge surge of peace. He did not want to dwell on the governor's words: "a life for a life." He drank whisky from the bottle; then he walked down the corridor when the door handle of Giuseppe's room loosened and the door opened slightly. A shadow fell through the gap, and he heard a long deep moan of pleasure. Elias carefully opened the door enough to put his head through to see the maid kissing his uncle frantically and then going on her knees to give him a blowjob. Giuseppe was sweating and cursing her and clutching her hair with both hands; he pushed her head further onto him. His body was scarred and tattooed, and something in what he saw brought Elias a flashback from his childhood when once he opened his parents' bedroom door to tell his mother something and saw her in pain, asking his father to stop penetrating her. The sight made him quickly close the door.

He stood outside the door, thinking about the mediocrity of human existence. How pathetic was that? Was this the normal slave-master relationship? Was she paid? He wondered how long this had been going on for. An hour later the maid left the room, not daring to look at Elias.

He was disgusted by his uncle's deceit and manipulation. He could take the private and constant scandals that he created in the town but not the ease and the alacrity of his lies. His insatiability puzzled him, from the restaurant owner to maids. True, deep inside Elias hated convention, but the abasement of a human being's feelings and desires disgusted him. Maybe he was foolish and wrong, but he was no longer sure of anything.

He stepped out into the night, heedless of the rain spattering his face. He felt alive for the first time in his life, relieved from a stupid guilt. People do what they want, he thought, and from that moment he decided that he would never owe anything to anyone anymore.

-+=● ●=+-

As the fish cooked on the fire, it gave off a strange smell. Elias and Giuseppe were drinking beer, sitting by the grill.

"Cheers," Giuseppe yelled.

"I can hear you. I'm not deaf," shouted Elias. "Cheers!"

"Oh! Someone's upset."

Elias wondered how to phrase what he needed to say and then said, "No, not at all."

"Do you want to talk about it?"

"I saw you yesterday having it off with the maid."

"And so?" A small muscle twitched in Giuseppe's face. "You were there all night, were you?"

"Of course not; I saw her going into your room. And what about Sally?"

"What about Sally? She lives hundreds of kilometres from here, and I am a man."

"Don't you believe in fidelity?"

"Bullshit! I only believe in personal happiness—whenever you can get it, grab it." His fierce eyes lit up like a fire.

"So your personal happiness is this maid?"

"Maid or not, if she can satisfy me, why not? Happiness is only moments; nobody remembers all his eighty years or one hundred. We only remember moments."

His chest was sagged and wrinkled. He was old yet Elias recognized Giuseppe still felt an unassailable need for love, myths, and dreams; his admissions were blatant and too personal not to be true. All his life he had sought recognition and echoes of love in women's arms. In the distance Elias saw the fabled railway stealing across the horizon. As a train passed by, he compared it to his life travelling on, never stopping at any destination for long. At some places, maybe no more than a few days; at others a bit longer. Every day a new scene, a new passenger, a new story or a new truth. You only knew that the train was moving forward when you saw the landscape running backwards. His life was like pages in a book, where each written page skipped past leaving space for a new script.

"I know you might find it unsettling, but I assure you, it won't change any-thing; don't read anything into it," Giuseppe said, looking concerned.

"You weren't going to tell me anything about it, were you?"

"I didn't want to worry you, that's all," Giuseppe was apologetic and abashed. "I don't tell you everything, you know; I don't want you to worry about me."

"Fair enough."

"OK, she was pregnant twice, but I made her abort."

"Why?"

"Because she is married for God's sake! You are a bit disappointed that I didn't keep the child? It is never easy whatever you do in these cases."

"You or both of you?"

"I don't think there is much to say about it; me or her it doesn't really matter. No need to overreact."

"Does Sally know about all of this?"

"Why should I tell her? I am sure she's making it with someone else too. We all have secrets, Elias, some darker than others."

"OK. Shall we go? It's getting a bit cold, and we have lots of packing to do."

As the day passed, it was liberating in some ways. When they reached the hacienda, Elias raised the subject again over dinner, trying his best to sound as relaxed as possible.

"Do you love Sally?"

"Love is like anything that's made to be consumed. I am a flame that has to burn," he said jokingly, a false cheeriness in his voice. "Then what do you mean by love? Of course I love her as I love you as I love anybody in my life. I have never hated anyone."

Elias was not sure he was convinced by this explanation, and he was also uneasy discussing this in front of the maids.

"Love is complicated. We don't love people per say, but we love how they make us feel. I feel great with Sally, but I don't think we could live together. She is too wise for me. I need more playful women." Then he stood up. "Please let's talk about this later. I need to go to bed."

When Elias looked in his eyes, he knew a moment of real dread. He realized Giuseppe might not live for long. Elias gave him an answering nod and realized the room felt more spacious after he'd left. Giuseppe was the kind of man who filled a space with his presence, but Elias realized he was at least able to hold a coherent conversation with him, something he could never do with his mother.

As the morning inched ever closer, Elias woke up on the sofa. He must have collapsed and fallen asleep. The household was still asleep. He looked in the mirror at his red-rimmed eye. He heard the postman deliver some letters. Elias flicked through them. One of them was addressed to him from Lebanon, so he opened it. As he read the contents of the letter, he slumped back down on the sofa, nodding dumbly, holding the letter with tears streaming down his cheeks. His father had just passed away. At that moment Giuseppe appeared at the door, and Elias turned to him his face, wracked with grief.

"I can hardly believe it," he repeated the sentence over and over. His sense of continuity just collapsed; his fractured life came back full of flashbacks, of rare moments of happiness, running with his brother along the sandy beach chasing his father. Giuseppe was powerless to help and looked at Elias, confusion in his face. He wasn't a man who could deal with emotions.

"My father died when I was four years old," he said. He bent down and kissed Elias's forehead. "I am so sorry for your loss. I liked your father a lot. He was such a kind and peaceful man especially as he put up with your mum. Will you have to go back?"

Elias was unaware of anything or any words. He felt edgy and restless within the confines of the house. He got shakily to his feet and left the room and walked into the garden. There he sat on the old wooden bench beneath a leafy tree and stared at a bird perched in front of him and peered into the distance. He wished he could be the bird; he wanted to fly as far away as he could. Moments later his uncle was sitting next to him on the bench, sliding an arm around his shoulders, drawing him up against him.

"Do whatever you want. If you want to go to Sally for a few days, don't hesitate; just tell me, and I'll arrange it."

A cold breeze ruffled his thick black hair, and he stared down the length of the garden with an expression that Giuseppe could not understand. Elias was in another dimension. He did not need just a few days but a whole lifetime, a newly created world where he could find his soul again. He was prepared to lose the world but not his father whom he loved with all his heart. Now he was a mess.

His hair stuck out at all angles; his eyes were red and blotchy from crying. Giuseppe sat in silence. He was crying too but stifled his tears; he didn't want to upset his nephew even more, but his heart was ripping out through his chest.

Elias opened his wallet and took out an old photograph of his father. "Some people say when you talk to someone's photo, you steal their soul; now I want to trap his soul forever inside my heart."

A strange feeling squirmed somewhere inside Giuseppe. He had never seen this photo. His sister used to send him news every week; then the letters became rare and suddenly stopped with the war. Suddenly and for the first time, he asked himself what he was doing here. His life was an accumulation of small pieces; he felt the need to pack up and leave everything behind but where could he go and who would he go to? He had been alone for so many years that he wouldn't be able to share his space with anyone, especially a woman—he found them too demanding. The idea of losing Elias was unbearable; he loved him like a son and couldn't think of living without him.

Inevitably conversation could not stray far from the event for the whole day. Clearly Elias was struggling with the idea of death and burial. How could he bury his father? He was so alive, loved people and his friends, and was so loyal to all those who loved him.

"Was he sick, Elias?"

"He had heart problems, and apparently after I left he had one minor heart attack in his bed, but the day before he dragged the body of a woman who had just been hit by a sniper. He didn't want her to die in the middle of the street."

"Why did you never tell me all this?" Giuseppe demanded, swivelling in his seat to look at Elias. "Each time you called your parents, I asked you if everything was OK, and you always answered yes."

"I'm sorry," he whispered. "Mum told me not to worry you."

"Ah, your mum; she always hid things from me even when we were kids. She always wanted to protect me from the world! Your father always seemed a rather distant and aloof figure, but I always liked him. Everyone in our family thought him rather a cold and remote individual, but I am sure he was kind and charming. He never put his job before his family."

Elias held his hand tight, and his tears kept falling. "I know he gave that impression but actually he was adorable—never hurt me even with a look. I feel so guilty that I left."

"You shouldn't! He wanted to protect you. He called me and asked me to take you away, even to confiscate your passport so you would never go back."

"Really? I thought Mum called you."

"No, he did; he was very worried. I'd never known him like that. He even offered to pay me his retirement money so I could look after you properly."

"Why does nobody tell me anything in this damn family?" Elias shouted in anger.

"In this instance he really insisted on me not telling you anything."

Elias was in pieces, unashamedly heartbroken, and nobody could lessen his pain.

Giuseppe stood up. It was almost twelve o'clock. "Do you want me to call the priest and ask him to say a mass tomorrow morning? Or do you want to go back to Lebanon to bury him? Think about it. I have to call your mother." Deep down Giuseppe didn't want Elias to go back; his throat went dry. Maybe it is me next, he thought. His heart started beating wildly.

Elias gave him a sad ghost of a smile. He was alone with his pain, and he seemed to have lost his world. Strangely enough he didn't feel the urge or the desire to go back to Beirut nor to see his mother. He felt driven by a burning need to be busy, to outrun his pain. He left the garden and went off to work with Diego.

The next day Giuseppe had a meeting in the house with local politicians. He was trying to get the local governor replaced by his rival. He was no good to him anymore, and the pressure to pay one million real to the governor's nephew was mounting. Giuseppe was beginning to tire of the governor's insistence. He needed to get on with his life.

Elias showed up and asked if he could join the meeting. Giuseppe agreed and proceeded to introduce him enthusiastically as his nephew and his favourite boy in the world. For his part, now that his father was gone, Elias had only his uncle as a father figure, so he was determined to look after him. He didn't want to see him lying still and silent in a casket. With that thought in mind, he determined to involve himself in his uncle's business and political affairs.

In one heated political meeting in the public hall of the mayor's office, a young candidate, a black-haired man with cool green eyes appointed by the committee, stood up. He was immaculately dressed and came from a local prominent family. He was also very young and outspoken. He was scathingly funny about his girlfriend's dress and openly refused to take the tie that she held out for him. He seemed very enthusiastic about his candidature.

He started his speech by publicly criticizing Lebanon, saying "You people are riddled with wars and cursed by religion. You never had any allegiance to your country. Nothing matters more than money; you lost your souls. You killed women, children, and old people in your dirty civil war. After destroying your country, you come here, and you bring your dirty politics in our country. You are trying to corrupt our souls as well, but we will never let you win; we will defend our values."

Elias turned red, but Giuseppe held his hand tightly as he was about to stand up. "Let him speak," he said, his cigar clenched in his teeth.

"I can't let him rubbish you like this in front of everyone!" Elias said.

Elias felt strange about everything now having moved to a different world. He felt uneasy about these war tales; his heart was beating fast. Why now? Why here? Does this kid know something? Frustrated, he sat down; he blinked sweat out of his eyes and stared at the boy, clenching his fingers.

"Don't worry about me; just sit. I will deal with it accordingly," said Giuseppe.

The young man added that it was true that the birth of civilization and the alphabet came from this region, and when Europe was in the Dark Age, the Near East was in a golden age in astronomy and the sciences. Yet since then the region had slipped into its own dark age.

"How do you deal with differences? By eliminating them. Look what you did to the Palestinians—you slaughtered them like sheep. Poor refugees; all this and for what? You don't have a sense of citizenship, and you define yourself by your religion. Then you come here in our country, and you decide to make the law, with the bribes that you inherited from the Ottomans. You have no national identity. The intransigent problem confronting governments is that your nation is deeply divided along religious lines. Your domestic politics are polarized along sectarian divisions between Christians and Muslims and then among Christians and Muslims themselves. How can we trust you? You're arrogant; you believe you descend from the Phoenicians—an old myth that you carry with you to impress people. As clever and tenacious you are, you don't make your own laws here. You should be punished for the killing of Andreas and…"

With these words Elias became frantic and pale. He reacted badly at the words "division" and "killing." It was as if his conscience was talking to him through this man. Elias became paranoid, why did the speaker look at him personally when addressing the crowd?

He got up and made his way through the crowd until he reached the young man and punched him, knocking him down to the floor. In the ensuing struggle, when the young speaker got up, the audience jostled around him frantically, trying to divide both men. Short of breath Elias was ordered to leave immediately. For a moment he just stood there shocked by the blood pouring from the young man. He didn't know how long he'd been standing there, gripping a glass so tightly he lost all feeling in his hand, until Giuseppe grabbed him.

"Your behaviour is unforgiveable. There was no reason for you to react like that. Are you out of your mind? You humiliated me. I won't tolerate such reactions; are you listening? You were hitting him too hard," Giuseppe said, his face contorted with fury.

Elias breathed in a long deep of lungful of fresh air, relishing the wind that rustled his hair and dried his sweat. "I'm sorry." he muttered.

"I know you were angry because of your father's death, but this doesn't explain your behaviour. Are you out of your mind? If he dies tonight, you are in big trouble. I cannot help you with this; do you understand?"

"Yes, I do. I don't know what happened."

"Well, you hit him so hard, and you wouldn't stop, although Diego shouted at you. Why fight? Why risk your life for a pretentious idiot!"

"Diego was there?" He felt his nails digging into the palms of his hands.

"Yes, he was, and you were blinded by rage," Giuseppe's voice hardened. "I really need to know what the fucking hell is happening here. Am I missing something? Lately your behaviour has become weird."

Elias wished for the first time in his life that he could erase his past and start from scratch. He could see the stiffening in Giuseppe's face. They were hunched in the back of a stinking cab, jostling through traffic in the dark streets through wind and rain back to the hacienda. Elias was scared; despite the freezing rain, the streets were full. The old man wanted answers, but Elias was unable to provide him with a rational one. Elias kept his head turned away and stared through the window. Lovers were huddling underneath umbrellas waiting for the rain to stop. Not daring to look at his uncle, he felt he couldn't own up to his dismal thoughts and said nothing. He kept staring out at the endless rows of street lights passing by. For him they represented the few glimpses of happiness in his childhood when his father used to tell him to count these lights and when he reached one hundred, they would reach home. The cab rolled forward, and a sullen silence reigned over both of them. When they arrived at the hacienda, they both stepped out into the night and were heading towards the archway when a maid ran up to Giuseppe.

"You have to call the governor," she said nervously and out of breath.

Giuseppe looked very worried. "OK. Ring him back for me," he said; then he disappeared into his office.

Elias was left in the living room, and he looked at the candelabras and felt a huge sadness.

Giuseppe reappeared looking a bit anxious, but he said calmly, "The guy suffered a broken rib and some cuts in his face. He is in the hospital, but the village is in a rage, and they are demanding compensation. His father is a local judge, and he is awaiting the recovery of his son before pressing charges against you. Are you satisfied? I still can't explain your behaviour. I told the governor that your father passed away and that you are feeling under pressure, but he doesn't seem to care. It's all politics. I don't know. What can we do? Anyway I'll call my lawyer tomorrow."

"I'm sorry, Uncle. I've put you in deep trouble." Elias felt his throat tightening up. "I don't know...but to see this arrogant man just tearing you apart was difficult to accept."

"Well, you have to learn to calm down in life; your father wouldn't have appreciated this kind of behaviour."

Elias shrugged sending droplets of water spraying from his coat onto the old red carpet. "I want to go to sleep," he said and made his way up the wooden staircase directly to his room. He kept his coat on and lay down on his chipped wooden bed and stared at the ceiling spanned with spider webs. He felt empty. He looked at the oil painting facing him of an English landscape; it was surrounded by sagging bookshelves lining the walls. The soot-stained fireplace and the cracked wrought-iron windows added to his sadness. The place was as fallen apart as his life. He missed his father badly and started crying.

The next morning Giuseppe woke him up with a lightened voice. "Come on son, time to wake up; it's almost eleven o'clock. The young guy is back home, all OK."

Elias didn't answer immediately; smiling a little he said, "Great news," before collapsing in the chair.

"Indeed. OK, maybe you need to go back to work."

"Yes, sure. I'll have breakfast—I'm starving; then I'll head back to work."

"OK, see you at dinner."

-->|■■() (■■|-<-

Days passed by, and things had seemingly returned to normal. Then one afternoon while Elias was working on the farm, he looked up and saw the maid running towards him, screaming, telling him to come back to the house. Giuseppe had been shot. Elias ran so fast that he almost collapsed as he reached the living room and saw his uncle lying on the floor in a pool of blood, his eyes wide open and staring into nothingness, his skin translucent. Elias struggled for breath; he couldn't believe what he was seeing. When he could breathe again, he asked the maid what had happened.

The maid, clearly terrified, said she'd heard two gunshots and ran to the living room to find Giuseppe lying there. Then she ran back to the open door in time to see the silhouette of a man running through the archway, but he was too far away for her to identify him.

Elias ordered her to cover the body with a white sheet. "Now!" he shouted as he saw her hesitate. There was nothing else he could do, so he just sat holding his uncle's cold hand and cried, howling in agony. Now he was alone in this world with two shadows: his father and his uncle. Shivering uncontrollably, he asked himself what would happen to him now. He feared the end had come at last—maybe it was his turn now? The voice inside him grew so loud that he closed both his both ears with his hands. The maids and workers were all around the body looking at each other in amazement, some of them making the sign of the cross, the men taking off their hats. From all over the hacienda, they came to pay him their respects. Some of them had known him for twenty years. Many spontaneously kissed his hand out of respect whereas others fingered their ears and had mixed feelings between fear and confusion. Elias did not know what to do, so he asked the maid to call the police and especially not to touch anything in the house. He could barely hear his own voice. What to do? he asked himself. What to do? He had nobody to turn to. He dusted himself off, stood up, and asked the men to help him put the body on the sofa. He held his uncle's blood-soaked head, and they laid him gently on the couch.

A little later the police came to the house and transported the body to the coroner's office. Elias had to accompany them. At the police station, Elias filed a complaint against the governor.

"You are accusing the governor of the murder of your uncle?" the policeman asked him.

"Yes. Surely there's something you can do about it."

"It is not up to us to decide."

"Up to whom then?"

"There are no witnesses; how can we accuse someone of a murder with no witnesses."

"He told me 'a life for a life' when I saw him at Margarita's." His voice sounded uncertain.

"Maybe, but that's not enough proof. The governor is a much respected man in this community. I really do advise you to pack and leave," the police said with an air of frustration but still keeping his expression impartial and curious.

"This is what you all wanted from the beginning, starting with that idiotic speech."

"Yeah, but the speechmaker—he was Lebanese descendant."

"Doesn't make it right though."

"Maybe not right, but he wasn't far from the truth," he said, staring at Elias, weighing and judging and inhaling on his cigarette. "I think it's time for you to go."

"It was an election gathering and a character assassination," Elias said and looked at his watch. It was one o'clock in the morning, and he needed to go and sleep. "I need to bury him first."

"Of course, we will arrange everything for you."

Elias headed to the farm, his thoughts racing. What could he have done to protect his uncle? In his room his clothes were strewn everywhere, scattered on the chair and the bed. He knew he couldn't win. Better let it go for the moment. Nobody believed him that the governor was behind the murder. People wanted to believe that Giuseppe had a struggle with a thief; nobody appreciated his obstinacy in the matter. He told Sally about Giuseppe's death and the funeral arrangements. She came the next day all dressed in black; there was something sad and unreachable behind her eyes. She couldn't understand why anyone would want to hurt Giuseppe. She stood on the balcony, smoking and staring at the horizon, wondering if she could convince herself one day that he had gone. She asked to be left alone in his room, and she sat on the edge of his bed, held his pyjamas, and sobbed. Down the hallway she heard the crackle and hiss of the radio with his favourite song, and she relaxed a little.

Elias knocked on the door, came in, and held her gently for a long time; she buried her face in his shoulder, and they both cried. Then Elias collapsed into the hard wooden chair near the bed. He closed his eyes, and his mind drifted to the first time he and Giuseppe met at the airport, and Giuseppe had seemed so happy to see Elias.

"When will the body arrive at the church?" Sally asked.

"Soon," he replied. "We should really get going; all the village will be there waiting for us, even the murderer. This world is so theatrical; don't you think so?"

"There'll be no investigating committee?"

"No, that's it; the case is closed."

"Now finally he can rest…I miss him so much," she said, staring back at him with her tired blue eyes. Slowly she blinked.

"Yes, me too, Sally," he said and realized he felt cold.

"You must come home with me," she said, her words coming out slightly slurred.

"I don't know. I haven't thought about it much. Do you really want me to go with you?"

"Where else would you go?"

"Well, all right; but not for long. What I really want is to be a painter," he confessed, staring upwards and realizing that she needed him in her life.

"An artist?" She looked at him completely astonished.

Elias sank back in the chair, exhausted.

"Yes," he said. "Do you know someone who can teach me?" He stared at her beseechingly.

After a while she said, "Yes, I do. One of my clients runs a drawing school. I'll ask him."

"Thank you," he tried a smile of gratitude, but it felt false.

"OK, let's go now," she said, getting up. They moved slowly to the door and headed downstairs.

Chapter II

ELIAS PUT THE farm up for sale. He couldn't deal with it and wanted to put the past behind him once and for all. Like the flickering candles in the hacienda, Giuseppe had dissolved into nothing. The case was closed, and the farm was sold to three people who divided the land.

Driving away that day in Sally's car, Elias thought about the banality of life and destiny. He was definitely on quite a different journey from where he'd started; he'd been shy, sad, and intimidated on his arrival driving from the airport in Giuseppe's car. Now, agitated and yearning for peace, he was a man who'd just lost his father and uncle, leaving them behind as memories. Life for him was a battlefield littered with ghosts, wicked souls, dissolved flesh, and carapaces from the past hunting him down. He was reminded of his neighbour, the daughter of Om Salma, run over by a car when she was six. She was left with a brain injury and post-traumatic stress disorder. She combated both with unparalleled courage, but after many operations and much suffering, she died at the age of thirty-four. He was left struggling to understand the meaning of life. He was now convinced that there was no big plan or destiny. It's pure chance that we are alive, he thought. The stronger ones manage to survive only to be crushed later. We are all butterflies attracted to light until it burns us, but it's the only choice we have. Life refuses to give away its secrets and only hints at a few things, which prompt us to go ahead, not knowing what to expect. Yet some roads are full of potholes, and some grassy fields hide bumps and crevices.

Sally respected his silence although he would catch her staring at him sometimes, but he was not in a mood to share his thoughts. At last he said, "How far will we go?"

"We have a long journey ahead. I'll try to go fast but not when we're passing through the villages. You can sleep a bit if you want," she said.

"I'm fine," he said. "I just want to relax and close my eyes."

"Meanwhile would you like me to stop at a bar so we can have a bite to eat and a drink?"

"Yeah, sure but not now." He couldn't help feeling irritated with her interruptions to his chain of thoughts.

He wanted to be alone and think about Giuseppe, and he didn't want to share his memories with anyone. He held him close to his heart and all the beautiful things that had happened with him in the hacienda. Giuseppe had lived life to the fullest far from people with their nonsense and beliefs. He'd been positive to the point of irritation. He'd loved his whisky, cigars, and beautiful women and enjoyed all his debaucheries without guilt. He'd always found a reason for everything he did. His presence alone could fill a room; now silence, the master of all words, replaced his existence.

From the car window, Elias could see people wandering on the sidewalks going from bar to bar. Natives and not tourists crowded the streets. Outside a cold wind shivered through the city, but it didn't seem to deter people from partying and drinking around fires. One man squirted a liquid from a bottle, and with the strike of a match, the fire blazed higher and louder, throwing sparks into the night. He compared his uncle to one of these short bursts of flames that shone a light for people in the darkest hours of their lives. One dies leaving space for others as if it was a transaction—one human being for another, a birth for a death, Elias thought. Suddenly he felt the need to be with these people to share his loss with strangers. He turned to Sally, and in a firm voice, told her to stop the car.

"Now?" she said. "Where? Here? There's nothing for us here."

"Yes, here."

She pulled the car over to the edge of a narrow street. He left the car and headed towards the crowd.

"Can I join you guys?" he called out.

They welcomed him with tired eyes. "Are you OK, kiddo?" one of them asked.

"I just lost my father and my uncle a few months apart."

They laughed uncertainly thinking he was fooling them. Their laughter was too shrill, their gestures too frantic. He wasn't afraid of them; he thought their smiling faces showed a certain restraint. Still all these drunken men singing and dancing did not move him. Poverty had shaped their bodies. They had black bags under their red eyes. They looked shabby and unhealthy, but they were probably happier than he was. He wondered what these shrunken old men thought about life. Some prostitutes stalking the streets joined the crowd with their cheap furs, slinky costumes, and broken high heels. One of them realized he was different, and she touched his crotch begging for love. He thanked her politely with a few coins and then left them and went to the nearby bar. There he ordered a whiskey and bought a cigar.

He sat in a corner. The barman looked at him curiously. "You're not from here; am I right?" he asked.

"No, I'm not," he answered, drinking the whiskey in one gulp. He gestured to the barman to refill his glass. "I came from far away, and I'm heading to Los Montes with my old mistress."

"Old? You are so young! How could you have an old mistress?"

"I stole her," he mumbled, "from my old uncle. Then when he was killed, I ran away with her. I'm a man of danger and seduction." He tapped his empty glass twice pointing to the bottle of whiskey. The barman poured for the third time. "I am a god of war and sex," he said, now completely drunk. "I killed a lot of people—a lot; I butchered them."

Sally left the car, angry now and looking for Elias. Ignoring the drunken crowd around her, she pushed her way through. A prostitute directed her to the bar, and as she entered through the small metal door, a smell of cigarette smoke, grease, and beer filled the air. She looked everywhere for Elias; then she heard his booming laugh resound over the noisy crowd. He was drunk and betting with the bartender—he emptied his wallet onto the table surrounded by miners and factory workers.

"Are you OK?" Sally rushed towards him in panic.

He stared at her and then laughed. "Are you rescuing me?" he asked. Gazing at the men around him, he lifted his glass and called out, "Cheers everybody."

"Yes, from yourself; you look pathetic. You're making a fool of yourself," she said, her hand on his arm.

"No, I was having fun with these nice people," he said, and then he laughed.

"What's this about then? The attention?" she asked angrily. "That's enough fun! We're going back home; we have a long road ahead."

Elias grinned slowly. "What do you think it is about? I want to stay here where I can forget my pain. Then I want to eat. I'm sure they'll feed me."

"I doubt it, and I can't do anything about it now as there is no decent restaurant here. I promise we'll stop in the next town, but you need to rest; you've had a hard day."

"You don't understand, Sally; these are my friends." Then he whispered something in his neighbour's ear and collapsed.

The crowd of miners, prostitutes, and thieves gathered around them, and she looked desperately at the tall flat-nosed bartender begging him to help her. He smiled a sadistic smile, nodded, and they both carried Elias to the car. He asked Sally for money to pay for the bottle of whiskey and for all the drinks that Elias had offered the crowd.

Sally gave him a despising look. "How could you allow this to happen? He's only a kid in grief; how could you take advantage of him?"

"Not my problem. I don't have charity written on my forehead. If the money isn't paid, I'm in trouble here, not you."

"Well, I don't have that amount in my purse."

"So give me your ring then; that'll do," he said in a menacing voice looking at her figure.

Sally felt he was a man of violence and action, and she knew she had no choice. She stared at his chest, then took off her ring, and gave it to him.

"Go to hell," she said, closing the car door on Elias. Then she got into the driving seat and drove away.

⇥⊙ ⊙⇤

Sally felt Elias's pain. She too missed Giuseppe. She remembered how Giuseppe had helped her with her grief over her daughter's death when she first met him on the train. They were in the same carriage, and he produced a cigar and began unwrapping it. He was smartly dressed, heading for the wedding of the son of his best friend, and he introduced himself as the king of the feast. They spoke listlessly at first, then with mounting enthusiasm as they got to know each other. When they left the train, he asked her to come with him.

Surprised by his offer, she demurred politely. "Are you sure this is wise?" she had asked. "I am not dressed appropriately, nor do I know these people."

Despite her irritation nothing seemed to bother Giuseppe. "You are with me," he answered. "No need to know the world. I'm enough," and he laughed.

After much hesitation she ended up at the wedding with him dancing all night long, and after that she couldn't leave him. He fascinated her although he was much older, and he had the power to make everybody laugh. He was alive, irresistible. Then towards the end of the night, she felt she had to kiss him.

"I want…" she began.

"Hold that thought," he said. "I'm going to look for some privacy." Then he carried her inside the house, up the fire escape, a narrow wrought-iron staircase, to the roof. He slowly put her on the floor, took off his tuxedo, and folded it into a cushion, and then laid her head on it and started kissing her. The wind was howling around them, and he had to shove his hat down his head.

In the far distance, the lights of the harbour glittered, and he showed her the secret garden behind the house. Looking down, she saw the scattered guests laughing, drinking, and talking loudly. They made their way down to rejoin the reception when his best friend, the groom's father, looked at Giuseppe.

"Hey, where did you disappear to?"

"I had to satisfy my woman, didn't I?" Giuseppe said, looking at Sally with a huge smile.

She squirmed with embarrassment. "Euh…in fact he wanted to show me your beautiful garden…"

"Let's drink to that then," the man said, and he burped.

The party after the wedding was lively; the guests and parents danced all night long. It was a merry, convivial scene. It was obvious that they were all a close-knit group, and she stared at them feeling nostalgic. She felt like someone missing a past she had never known. Giuseppe was the opposite of her father; he knew how to enjoy life and how to make people around him enjoy it. He looked so handsome with his white silk tie, and when he approached her and stuck a little flower in her hair, he made her look stunning. He stopped for a moment; their eyes met, and he grabbed her round the waist and said, "God, you are beautiful! Thank you for coming."

She went home in the early hours of the morning, completely shattered but extremely happy and satisfied. She thought it was impossible to love anybody more than she loved him. At the beginning they met quite often. She would take the train to see him for a day or two. Then he was caught up with politics and could not see her more than once a month. Then her visits became rarer. She suspected he was seeing other women, but she couldn't leave her hotel as she had debts to pay and moving to his side of the country was too big a change for her. As the years passed, she heard little from him until Elias arrived, and he called her again. He probably needed help with the kid, but she could not refuse him, and she accepted his invitation and came.

"Haven't heard from you in a while," she said.

"I apologize for that, but you could have phoned me too."

"True, but I thought maybe you had someone in your life by now."

"You know me. I am a tough old bachelor. I've also been very busy with local politics. They needed my help, and I need to ask you a favour."

"Please do," she said and paused, letting out a small inaudible sigh.

"My nephew is arriving tomorrow, and I need your help and advice. You know he was engaged in the militia and his father wanted him to leave to spare his life."

"Sure, do you want me to accommodate him?"

"No, I need him here, but thank you for offering. You know my world lacks the feminine touch, and it would be great if you could meet him."

"When do you want me to come over?"

"I don't know yet. I need him to settle here first. What about in a month or two?"

"OK, that'll give me time to organize someone to replace me."

"Are you still beautiful? Giuseppe asked. "A hot ass?"

"I don't know about that; you'll have to judge for yourself."

He laughed.

"Don't get too excited," she said.

He gasped suddenly unable to speak.

"What is it, Giuseppe?"

A silence came down the phone.

"I'm sorry I've neglected you lately," he said in a low voice.

"Don't worry. Things happened, and we have different lives. I still think about our first dance. I wished it could have lasted for ever."

"Yes, true; it was a beautiful time."

"OK. I'll get back to you. Call me in the meantime if you need any help."

"OK. Love you."

"Love you too, Giuseppe."

Remembering these last words, she choked and woke Elias.

"Are you OK?" he said.

"Yes, I'm sorry I woke you. How did you sleep?"

"Oh, deeply. I feel much better but very hungry."

"OK, we'll stop in fifteen miles or so; there's a nice restaurant with a breath-taking view."

"It doesn't matter; it's almost the middle of the night."

"Yes, of course. Anyway I know the family well, and they'll have some bread and soup for us I'm sure, Elias."

"Great."

After about fifteen miles, Sally stopped the car, and they both headed to the restaurant, which had a huge neon sign over the doorway, saying *El Delicio del Alma*. She rang the bell, and an old woman appeared, her brown hair speckled with white, her face heavily wrinkled, yet the years had not taken the sparkle from her eyes. At the sight of them, she stuck out her bottom lip and peered at them in surprise.

"Sally, is it you? What are you doing here? Is everything OK?"

"Oh yes, thank you. I am here with…" she gestured towards Elias. "It's a long drive back home, and I thought I'd stop here with my nephew. We wanted to have soup and some bread; would that be possible?"

The old woman stood aside to let them in. "Of course come in, but you know it is so late. I'll bring you what's available. Please take a seat over there."

She directed them to a table with a view of the valley. Only dim lights from far away gave a sense of an irresistible beauty and calm.

"Does this suit you?" asked the old lady.

"Great!" Sally answered. Then the old lady disappeared into her kitchen.

With a raised eyebrow, Elias asked Sally why she introduced him as her nephew.

"She's old and traditional and wouldn't understand that you might be my…"

"Your what?"

"My…I don't know how we should call ourselves." Her cheeks flushed.

"Your lover, do you mean?" said Elias, rubbing his jaw.

"Yes, that suits me." She passed her hand over her face. Maybe deep down she wished she was twenty years old. She could feel her wrinkles and could even count them.

The old lady came in with a big tureen. "Here, my sweethearts, hope you like the soup. I made it today very fresh from the parsnips I grow in the little garden behind my kitchen." Then to Sally's immense frustration, she sat down with them.

The old lady had been lonely ever since she had been widowed. She started chatting with Elias and then looked perplexed. Sally knew why, of course. The old lady realized that Elias was not her nephew.

"No problem, love," she told Sally. Then she pulled up her chair and turned her back and headed towards the counter. "I'll read a newspaper and wait for you to finish eating."

They both ate silently and then left as soon as they'd finished, thanking the old lady. Back in the car, Elias leaned against her, and she welcomed the comfort of his arms. He asked about the old lady. Sally explained that she'd worked for her father for years and then retired with her husband and bought this place.

Sally had never felt this way before. Elias seemed to have awakened the tiger inside of her; she acted as if she was five. She wanted him for herself, and the idea of him living in her hotel gave her peace of mind. He'd be away from the flirty girls in town, but his desire to move back to town made her very uncomfortable. Hopefully he would forget about it, she thought. Then she cried, making her mascara run, and she wiped her face with her hand.

"Are you OK? Tell me what happened, Sally," Elias said, cradling her head.

"Sorry." She sniffed and pulled away. "Too many losses lately, that's all. Giuseppe wasn't only a friend but a father figure too," she said.

"I know what you mean. Do you want me to drive so you can relax a bit?"

"No, it's fine; I need to think about something else. It's all too upsetting, and we're not far away; in fact we've almost arrived."

"I can't wait to see your hotel. Giuseppe talked about it so much."

"It's my hub, and besides I love my customers; they're all different from different backgrounds and nationalities."

"Oh, and don't forget to call your artist friend."

"No, I won't. He doesn't live far, and he always asks my permission to paint in my garden."

"That's great," Elias said.

"But why an artist? Why not something else?"

"I don't know. I've always been fascinated by art, but my mum wouldn't let me enrol in any art classes. She was too embarrassed to tell her friends. You know, in Lebanon you have to be a lawyer or a doctor; anything else means you've failed."

"Oh, I see! But you won't earn a lot. You know that, don't you?"

"With the sale of the farm, I have some savings—although it went for less than it was worth; nobody wants to live in a house where a murder's been committed."

She nodded her head slowly. "I have been saving up, so if you want any help to set up a gallery or a showroom, just ask me."

He smiled and kissed her on the cheek. She glanced at her watch. Another twenty minutes to go. Her heart skipped a beat, and suddenly she felt a bit foolish, but she touched his hand. Twenty minutes later they arrived, and Sally got out of the car and rang the bell beside the double wrought-iron gates. A figure appeared in the dark and opened them, and she drove down a driveway lined with trees and pulled up behind a big house.

Elias could barely see in the moonless night but heard the bellboy arrive breathless after running all the way to take the luggage.

As Sally put the key in the lock of the front door, her heart was pounding. She knew deep down that this dream would not last, and once Elias was living with her, there was no way back. One day she would have to let him go. She felt drained physically and emotionally by the day's events.

"Please feel at home, Elias," she said once they were inside. "Pour yourself a whiskey; the bar is over there. I'm going to soak myself in a bath."

His eyes met hers, and they held each other's gaze for a moment although her eyelids were heavy with exhaustion. He hesitated and then poured himself a cognac instead.

"I will wait for you here," he said. She nodded and disappeared up the stairs. Elias sat down, exhausted. He lit the fire, as the house was freezing, and he was on his third glass when she appeared, feeling better. She sat on the sofa next to him, and they started kissing. She closed her eyes. He pulled her into his arms and followed her lips instinctively. She put down his glass, and then he grabbed her firmly towards him, forcing his tongue into her mouth, licking her gums. She nearly retched and pleaded with him to stop, but he continued with even more force.

"Let's go to my room," she said.

"Where is it?"

"Upstairs on the right."

"OK." He held up her hand. "I love your house—so neat and tidy."

They went slowly up the stairs, and she smiled. "I like it that way."

Her bedroom was opulent and spacious. Her big oak bed stood in the middle, surrounded by linen cloth to prevent mosquitoes in the summer. A sheepskin carpet lay on the stone floor in front of the bed. A deer's head jutted out from one wall, and a pair of shooting rifles hung on the other wall. It was an unusual lady's bedroom. Two tall tallow lamps burned on the side table; some portraits were scattered around the room—photos of a little girl with her father. She was in a white dress and him as a hunter figure on his knees hugging her.

Elias sat on the edge of the bed, waiting for her to come out from the bathroom. She came to him utterly naked; she lifted her foot and shoved it down on his chest, pushing him into the mattress. He struggled to breathe once she was on top of him.

"You look very nervous," she said.

He looked at her and pushed her on her side and then stood up, took off his pants, and went on top of her, spreading her legs.

"I am the man here," he said in a sharp voice. "In bed you belong to me; we aren't equal."

She licked her lips and swallowed and then kissed him, moaning; her body tensed, and her breathing stopped. She fixed him with a hungry stare. He couldn't resist her. Slowly, with exploring hands, he caressed her long, thin body, kissing her passionately.

"I want to keep you as long as possible," she muttered.

-->==◉ ◉==<--

Sally woke up at three in the morning. She couldn't sleep, and she wasn't sure whether it was because of Elias snoring or because of what happened earlier that night. Nevertheless she was in good spirits and thought the whole evening had passed off rather pleasantly. She sneaked to the bathroom without switching on the light, as she didn't want to disturb Elias. For a moment she turned to look at him and admired his young naked body tangled with the white sheet around his waist. He looked like a Greek warrior, taking a deep breath before going off to another victorious battle. He was so handsome. With this sad thought, she closed the bathroom door behind her, and with the dim light above the basin, she found her way to the toilet seat, which she closed and sat on and cried. She refused to look in the mirror in front of her. In her opinion mirrors never flattered anybody. The doctor had insisted she had to have a hysterectomy, but how could she? Her constant bleeding had become an embarrassment. The more she resisted looking at the mirror, the more she was drawn to it. Finally she glanced at the mirror. She was old and her hands so wrinkled, and with the shadows she looked one hundred years old.

How many times had she told Sophia, her greatest friend, how much she admired Elias and that there was still much of him to discover?

But Sophia argued against the relationship.

"Wake up! You are not going to marry him!" Sophia said constantly.

"No, I know I'm not," said Sally, annoyed.

"So what's the issue then?"

"No issue; I…want…just want him to stay a bit longer. I mean, for a while. He is a great lover."

"How many times have you made love? Then you can't expect him to stay for a while. He is less than half your age. Certainly he's agreeable, I give you that, but you are hurting yourself."

"Each time I visited the hacienda, we managed to make love…well, Agatha Christie married someone much younger than herself."

"Yes, but he loved someone else in the end; it's just natural…whatever you do, conceal your affection, or he'll run away from you. It's too much pressure on him. Look, Sally, I know. This does not make sense; please, I don't want you to be hurt."

"I think I am in love, Sophia."

"I know you are."

"How do you know? Is it so obvious? Do you think he suspects something?"

"I don't know about that; I don't know if men suspect anything!"

She liked Sophia. Although they were opposite characters, they were close. Nobody else in her circle liked Sophia. She was too blunt. She had herself been through many failed relationships in the past, and she had no faith in human love; when the affair finished she always walked away.

"Time is counted like money; what you use never comes back. When you look at photos, how many times do you realize that you forgot these moments? You know why? Because it flies by, and if you live in the past, you miss the present. The same if you dream about the future—you skip the present," Sally had said at the time.

She shook off these negatives ideas of Sophia and thought about what had happened in the bed when Elias became very impatient with her being too slow to come and the painful sex.

"You should do something about it," he said. "Each time I touch you, you are in pain."

She had run to the toilet and used some Vaseline and then came back, but the momentum was gone, and Elias had lost interest. He had already put on his T-shirt and sat on the edge of the bed. What to do? she thought. This was the only thing she wanted in life, a nice man by her side.

"You seem distant," Sally had said.

"Here we go again," Elias said. "Are you angry?"

"No, it was just an observation."

"What is 'just an observation'?"

"Well I don't know…I see you sad and distant."

"I am just bit on edge, that's all. I miss Giuseppe, that's all. He was quite a character, and I feel a void in my life, that's all; nothing personal."

Deep down Sally was worried that Elias felt guilty about his uncle, and now that he had died, all the passion, secrecy, and betrayal had faded.

"Everything in this house reminds me of him—the guns, the wine, even you."

"I can't deny it," said Sally. "We had great times; our paths crossed but not for long. You know, Elias, it is very hard to say this, but I love you. I never got this serious about anybody before."

Elias jumped and went to the hallway.

"I need a drink—a glass of wine, if you don't mind…don't wait for me. Just sleep. I'll be back," he said, looking apologetic.

She held her breath and rubbed her hands over her face for a second, trying to gather her thoughts.

Wait. Oh my God, didn't Sophia tell me to conceal my feelings? What have I done? she thought. She put on her robe and wanted to run behind him; then she stopped. I shouldn't, she thought, and she forced herself to stop. She leaned down on her chair in disbelief. That's it! I ruined it as I have ruined everything in my life! I'm my own worst enemy! Then she opened her drawer and took some pills to calm herself and waited for him to come back. Past two o'clock she had heard him come into the room, knocking against the chair near the door. She knew he was drunk, and she pretended to be asleep.

Back in the bathroom, Sally's thoughts returned to the present. She felt very tired not only physically but also emotionally drained. She tried to recover her composure and opened her white robe, unveiling her sagging breasts. She nodded. That's easily reparable when I do the hysterectomy. I'll do a breast job. I'll replace them with a beautiful pair, she thought. Her grin softened to a smile. She slowly walked back to the bed, and she pushed Elias's hand out of the way and tried to sleep.

Chapter 12

ELIAS SETTLED INTO Sally's hotel. She would work in her office all day long, and they would only meet in the late afternoon. As his birthday was approaching, Sally planned a big surprise for him. She asked her friend Vincenzo, the artist, to come to a garden party. Vincenzo was in his early fifties and extremely charming, his company a pleasure to others. He wore his naturally blond hair streaked with white, short except for a comb-over covering his baldness. He looked like the actor Omar Sharif, Sally thought. He was a successful artist, and most of his paintings were displayed at the National Museum of Modern Art in San Diego, Chile. He had divorced his wife and left his two daughters behind in Chile and moved to Brazil to be with the love of his life, a divorced mother of four. Tonight he was wearing his usual attire of jeans with a casual top.

"Hello, darling," Sally threw herself into his arms.

"Hi, gorgeous. Long time no see. Sorry, Elena apologizes, but she couldn't make it tonight. So what do you think of my jeans?"

"You look great," Sally lied; she had expected him to come better dressed to a garden party.

"I have to introduce you to one of my best friends, Elias. He's Lebanese, and he wants to be an artist."

Vincenzo turned towards Elias. "Oh, hi! Nice to meet you. I have lots of Lebanese friends. So you want to be an artist?"

"I need you to help him with some lessons," Sally interrupted.

"Yes," Elias replied to Vincenzo.

"OK, you have to visit my studio one day, and then we can discuss how to organize lessons."

As the waiters served drinks, Sally invited her guests to dance the salsa. After three shots of tequila and a vodka lemon, Vincenzo was tipsy. He looked around and then turned to Elias with a naughty smile in his shiny green eyes.

"Let's go to dinner tomorrow night. My girlfriend is hot and gorgeous, and I'll tell her to bring a friend of hers along so we can celebrate the beginning of your career. I'll come and pick you up around six?"

"That would be great," Elias replied.

After the party, as the hotel staff were cleaning up, Sally reached for a drink as the server was passing by with a huge tray.

"Ah, I want this one," she said and pointed at the glass of champagne.

"Of course!" the server replied.

She drank it swiftly and then turned towards Elias. "Did you enjoy the party? You spent your time with bunch of girls; you didn't even talk to me!" Sally blurted out, slurring her words slightly, and then looked at Elias directly. "You know you are mine!"

"No," said Elias, shaking his head. "I am not yours, nor anyone else's."

"Not mine?" The question sounded ridiculous on her lips.

"Come on, Sally; you need to sleep."

"This is making me mad, and I really don't want to be angry with you," she said and then left, and Elias followed shortly after.

-->==◎ ◎==<--

The next day the bell rang, and Elias opened the door with an easy smile.

Vincenzo greeted him. "Hi."

"Hello, Vincenzo, nice to see you; do you want to come in?"

"No, we have to go. I have people in the car. Are you ready?"

"Yes, I'm fine; let me just take my jacket."

Once inside the car, Vincenzo introduced him to both Elena and Ella. He bent and slightly kissed both girls' cheeks. They drove along the twisted coastal road. Elena was sitting next to Vincenzo on the front seat while Elias sat in the back with Ella. Elias was stunned by Ella; he had never seen such a breathtaking beauty. She looked tall with beautiful olive skin and big blue eyes, a slim figure with beautiful, generous breasts. He couldn't take his eyes off her, although he could not tell whether it was a fleeting physical attraction or much more.

After half an hour's drive, they arrived at a tapas restaurant. Vincenzo turned to Elias. "This is the best restaurant in Brazil," he said with a slightly amused smile. Vincenzo had booked the table with a view across the valley. Elena and Ella commented on the romantic setting, with the river below and the rolling green hills in the distance. Clumps of wildflowers were scattered across the pasture that ran down towards the river.

Elias timidly started a conversation with Ella. "So are you from here?"

"No. I am from Rio."

"What brought you so far?"

"Work. I'm a stripper."

"I see," said Elias. "Where do you work?"

"Actually funnily enough not very far from here, in a local bar."

"And you?" said Ella.

"I come from even further away than you. I am Lebanese."

"What brought you here?"

"The war and my uncle—long story. So are you married?" asked Elias, gazing down to her lower lip.

"That's going straight to the point! No, I have never been married, but I was with someone with whom I have a five-year-old daughter, but we are separated."

"So how long have you been separated?"

"When I fell pregnant," Ella replied.

"And your daughter lives with you?" He forced a tight smile.

"Yes, she does. I don't want him to see her; he's a very violent guy."

"Is he still bothering you?" Elias asked nervously.

"Sometimes, if he knows I am seeing someone else."

"I see," said Elias.

There was more than admiration and compassion in his answer. So he asked with a false cheery smile, "And are you seeing someone now?"

"You definitely don't lose time. No," she answered.

Then with no warning or hint, he pulled his chair closer to her and brushed his lips against hers. She moved slightly back.

Vincenzo and Elena raised their wine glasses. "Cheers," they both said.

Elias and Ella both laughed. "Cheers!"

There was a slight pause, and Elias could visualize her dancing at the pole and giving her body to him. Her presence had a visceral effect on him; he wanted to be with her alone. He reached out and held her hand, and she just surrendered it to him. Elias took Ella's phone number, and the following day he and Vincenzo met in his studio.

"So you seemed stunned by Ella."

"She is beautiful," said Elias.

"Forgive me for asking, but what is your relationship with Sally?"

"She is my mistress."

"I see. So what will you do now? You don't have any other accommodation or job. Sally is offering you all this, so you have to be careful."

"I know, so what do you advise me to do?"

"First we get the lessons done, and then we think about something, but if you want to see Ella, it should be serious. I like her a lot, and she is like a sister to me and the best friend of my girlfriend, so I don't want you to hurt her."

"I won't. How could I hurt her? I think I am already in love with her." said Elias.

"Be careful of her ex. He is a nutcase and dangerous. He won't let you touch Ella and his daughter."

"I'm up to it," replied Elias.

Elias became obsessed with Ella, coming to the bar every night to watch her. During the day, he worked with Vincenzo in his studio, producing tens of sketches.

"Do you think I'll be a good artist?" he once asked Vincenzo.

'You know it's not up to me to answer; art is not mathematical—it's just you."

"Yes, but what about technique? Surely it matters?"

"True, and that you can master. You can easily draw a profile, but you have to put life into it."

->==⊙ ⊙==<-

After leaving Vincenzo's studio, he would walk to the bar where Ella worked. One evening, through the darkness of the narrow street, a figure approached him.

"Get away from her." A tall man grabbed him by his collar. "Or I'll break your neck." It was clearly Ella's ex-boyfriend, and he stood in front of Elias with a menacing expression.

"Get off me," said Elias, his face contorted with anger and loathing.

"This time is OK. Next time I will kill you," the man said showing him his pocketknife; then he disappeared like a shadow.

Elias adjusted his shirt and walked towards the bar. He entered completely shaken by the incident. "Double whisky!" he called to the barman. He drank his glass and stared at Ella. After she finished she sat with him as usual at the bar, and he told her what happened.

"You have to watch him," she said. "He's not well. He can't accept the fact that it's finished between us."

"OK, look, I'm not scared of him. I'm just worried that he could harm you and the little girl. That's why I'll take the back door to come and see you, and we should both leave by the back door every night."

"Nothing to worry about; I know him. He's threatened me in the past but never did anything," she answered leaning on his shoulder. "We go? I'm exhausted."

"Yes, let me just ask for the bill."

→═◉ ◉═←

Elias looked out of the window and a rush of memories tumbled out. He missed Giuseppe; here he felt he was a stranger although Sally had everything arranged for him, even his personal butler, but still Elias felt lonely. He rushed out quietly, left the house, and walking towards the garden, he tried to imagine where Giuseppe was now. He thought a phenomenal woman like Sally does not deserve to be with someone whose mind was elsewhere. Right now he could not give her the full attention she needed. He wished he hadn't developed a sexual relationship with her. That was wrong of him, but he didn't know how to amend it.

Rather it was a struggle for him; she expected so much from him. Then there was the age gap; he found it difficult to kiss her sagging breasts. He needed youth and beauty.

"Elias?" Sally's voice curled around him.

"Yes," he turned, surprised. "Is everything OK?"

"Oh yes; I just saw you from the window of my office and thought I'd walk with you a bit. Do you mind?"

"Oh no. It's just so weird because I never see you during the day."

"Ah, don't worry. Nothing to do today."

"I see."

They walked a little way through the garden; then suddenly from somewhere behind them came Vincenzo, out of breath.

"Elias! Gosh, I was screaming your name, and you kept walking," he said, panting.

"Oh, I'm sorry; we didn't hear you," Elias apologized.

"OK," said Sally. "I'd better go and do some work. See you tonight then." She kissed Elias on the lips. Elias watched her silhouette disappearing behind the bushes.

"Are you OK?" Vincenzo asked.

"Yes…sort of. I'm still looking for serenity, but I can't find it today."

"Why?"

"I'm scared. I've tried to turn the page and move forward, but I haven't succeeded. I'm embarrassed to admit it. Wish I was laughing more; I'm trying but have to fake it a bit right now."

"I know; I can help you. I can feel your loss and pain, Elias, but what is really troubling you?"

"I am just thinking of the banality of all this."

"Death?"

"Our mundane life. What is the reason for life?"

"Are you religious?"

"I am not sure. Maybe, but that makes it even harder."

"You have the benefit of a higher reason."

"And yet faith is an even more difficult challenge."

"I won't give you an answer because it's not comforting, because it's irrational."

"Faith?"

"Yes, Elias."

"What about faith in life? What about the physical organic matter?"

"In a rational or irrational way, life just is, and you can try and make it good by your own standards. You know a colleague of mine goes off every night to sleep on the tops of mountains."

"Really?"

"She's up there alone tonight."

"So she can be close to God or the stars?"

"Nature."

"It takes guts."

"Yes, she started two weeks ago."

"But why?"

"Because she loves it."

"In a tent I suppose?"

"No tent; under the stars. Yes, it's irrational, but it gives meaning to her life."

"But aren't we all different and unique?"

"Yes, I think so."

"So what about inauthenticity? At least she is authentic to herself."

"Yes, she is, I agree, but conforming is an odd thing; we need to build a culture, a norm."

"For you being authentic means conformity?"

"No, the opposite, Elias."

"Ah, and how? Explain it to me."

"But what I'm saying is that I'm not sure the answer is that easy."

"For Sartre we have to be true to ourselves, not hypocrites," Elias interjected.

"Yes, but we are not alone, Elias."

"Yes, exactly; this is the point!"

"So how do we allow our acting to relate us to others?"

"We shouldn't act; we should walk away, as I should be doing here instead of lying to myself and staying with Sally."

"A friend has written to me today. Last year he was about to marry, and he was looking for a new life for himself and his wife in Sao Paolo. One week before marrying, he said 'I am not marrying you, and fuck everyone I am not coming back.'"

"He's right!"

"Yes, but he came back crying. He missed everyone, so be careful, Elias. You have everything here, and she is offering you the world; be careful. Think carefully. This guy thought he'd betrayed the people he loved."

"I don't know. I have to try. I came too far just to sit here in the shadows of this garden."

"It seems you've already made your decision, but whatever you do, don't hurt her. She doesn't deserve it; she's had a hard life, and she really cares about you. I have never seen her so happy before."

"I know, but I have to walk away," said Elias. He felt a sense of relief as he walked.

-->|==◉ ◉==|--

Sally was only too aware of the years that separated them. She knew she could never keep him forever. He was like a bird that needed to fly.

Her eyes brimmed with tears. "I will miss you," she said.

"I will come back for a visit, I promise," Elias said.

She wanted to open her mouth to shout and scream, but no sound would come out. She had steered clear of relationships unless they were casual. She didn't want to be hurt anymore; she didn't want to be emotionally attached.

"Can I do something for you before I leave?" Elias asked.

"Besides staying away from me? No, it's all fine," she answered, smiling weakly.

She was desperate for reassurance but fearful of what he might say. Elias could feel her dilemma, so he just left in silence. At the same time, he felt guilty, especially after the upheaval she'd experienced in her life. She kept looking at him as he walked away with his luggage. She knew that another woman was the cause of his leaving, and probably, she thought, if she hadn't come along, then maybe Elias would have stayed.

Chapter 13

ELIAS MOVED TO a small flat near Ella just after he started selling his paintings in the local market. On her day off, they would walk together in the local park or go for an ice cream.

"The weather today is cloudy," she said one day.

"Ah! Sweetheart, there is no kiss as gentle as that of a warm summer breeze across your neck. It makes me think of how you embrace me, and I savour the moment."

"The problem is I don't know what I want and who I am," she said.

"They say that a new chapter in a person's life cannot begin until the previous one is over. I think this oversimplifies the complexities of human communication. Ella, everyone wants to be heard, and the people closest to us are always competing for our attention. It's like a nest full of young crows, beaks agape all squawking incessantly for their demands to be gratified. The skill, my love, is to teach yourself not to hear their self-serving demands and instead focus on your own voice and ultimately decide what you truly want in life. Then you'll clearly see your goal and ultimately find your own happiness. Until you learn to turn away from the demands of those people closest to you, your own voice will be a whisper in a storm. I feel your pain and confusion, my love, but you must learn that true contentment lies within your grasp; you just have to turn in upon yourself to discover it."

"I don't know what I want or who I am, Elias. I don't want to be a stripper anymore. I'm tired of dancing and leaving my daughter alone every night. I'm sick of this confined existence in a cage where everybody can see my nudity."

"Let me explain what I mean, my love. Every day I used to swim a hundred lengths in Sally's pool. When I got into this pool, I'd take with me all the noise of the outside world, and initially, the first twenty or so lengths were laboured because my thoughts were still focused on other issues. After fifty lengths I started to concentrate more on my swimming, the length of my stroke, my breathing, and my rhythm. Eventually my focus turned totally on my progress through the water, and I became aware of the light dancing off the blue tiles. I could feel the water as it flowed across my skin, and I tasted every full breath of air. When I finished my swim and stepped out of the pool, I found I was totally focused on how I felt. I noticed how colourful my surroundings were, I could feel my heart pounding, and the world seemed richer, more welcoming. This is what I mean by turning in on yourself—it's a state of mind when the only thoughts that occupy you are about your own state of being. It's not meditation but more a case of funnelling your senses away from other people. That's when I feel more at ease and relaxed. I try whenever I can to find ways of recreating a chance to focus on my needs, my desires."

⇥✦⟞ ⟝✦⇤

Ella's childhood in Rio had been a tough one—her father died when she was eight, and her mother, not knowing what to do with six children, gave her away to her grandmother, who raised her in poverty. She was a good woman, but she was drunk most of the time. She used to invite her male friends home and then fall asleep, collapsing on her bed, totally drunk, leaving them alone with Ella. They would throw themselves on the young girl with their yellow teeth and dirty smell and rape her repeatedly, with raucous whispers in her ear about what a nice little girl she was. She was silent throughout the ordeal—she never screamed, resisted, or complained; then they would button their shirts and pants and leave the house quietly. She would fix her eyes to the ceiling with tears dropping along her cheeks, their semen tarnishing the old ripped bed sheets. It would take her long before she would drag herself to the shower. She used to run the water for as long as she could. The water and her tears blended. Her grandmother was never aware of her drinking pals abusing the little girl, and the next morning she would go to work as usual to clean public toilets.

When Ella reached fifteen, the local bar owner spotted her. She was terrifyingly beautiful with long smooth hair and a beautiful body. He picked her up in his car one day and convinced her to work as a pole dancer. She accepted, as she always did whatever was offered to her. She needed to blank out the soiled past with another soiled future. She said good-bye to her grandmother and moved out with her belongings in one plastic bag. She did not even want to see her mother or her siblings again.

The bar owner introduced her to the other dancers and gave her the clothes she should wear on stage. The wage was not that great, but tips were allowed, and if she encouraged a customer to drink, she would get her cut. Roberto, the bar security guard, used to look at her every night; she could sense him, feel him like smoke in the mist. One day he followed her to her small rented room above the bar and practically raped her, but she enjoyed his beautiful body and his muscles. At least he was better looking and much younger than the men she was used to. Lying on her bed, palms up, she just closed her eyes and didn't resist him. She was astonished at herself; she felt neither pleasure nor disgust. While he was moaning, she imagined herself running in a field of tulips, with a beautiful silk dress, nonchalant and free.

He lay a long time next to her. "You're so beautiful," he said and repeated it again and again. She looked at her naked body reflected in the mirror in front of her bed. She jolted back to reality, stood up, put her T-shirt on, and asked him to leave her room immediately. Then she sat and looked around at her old painted room, with the brown dirty carpet and started crying. What was she going to do? She remembered the manager's words: "If you're pregnant, you'll lose your job!" When she discovered she was pregnant, she told the manager about Roberto, who was dismissed the next day. As she was his best dancer, he allowed her to continue, providing her baby did not interfere with her job. Relieved and grateful she worked every night for long hours so she could afford help for her daughter and until she could afford to move into a bigger room in lodgings nearby.

She refused to see Roberto again; she resented herself for liking him and desiring him. She struggled to understand why she wanted him to rape her again. Maybe because this is the only thing she knew; she enjoyed the feeling of being desired and possessed even against her will. He found a job in the bar next door and stalked her every night. Meeting Elias was the best thing that ever happened to her. When Vincenzo told her that Elias had inherited from his uncle and that he was starting a new career, she presumed that in order to survive on your art, you must be rich.

Sitting in front of Elias in their favourite restaurant, playing with her broken nails, Elias said, "People are taught to read, write, and to do jobs but not to live."

"True," she said. "I love your philosophy." Then her gaze fixed on her hippie bracelets.

"Not taught how to cope with the crazy tragedy that life can be," Elias went on.

"Tell me about it," she said sadly.

"Tragedy and comedy," he muttered. "I said to a friend of mine yesterday that life is a Greek tragedy where you lose hopes and aspirations, but she didn't understand, and she told me I hadn't read them! I don't need to! It is all in Greek myths."

"True, true." She looked at him with her deep-blue eyes. Deep inside she was bored from his discourse.

"And Greek myths are my roots," he said.

"Where to begin in this life? Sometimes I think the ending is important, as the beginnings are always good." She smiled.

He looked at her and held her hands. "You always remind me to think; sometimes I forget to think."

"But really, Elias, don't you think so? That it's more rewarding to see the endings? That's where you see if you stood up to the challenges or not."

"Well," he said, "as someone who hasn't resolved his relationship with death, I take your comment with trepidation."

"I think both life and death are intertwined; they are just two sides of the same coin."

"I fear the end," he said then. "Yes, that's quite possible."

"I was really talking about the end of life where everyone speaks about your achievements. Don't fear death, as the beauty of it is you don't feel it when it happens."

"You are making me face my limitations, Ella."

"I'm sure you're up to it, Elias; don't put any limitations on yourself. Don't! Then you won't reach the sky and your dreams. You are a free soul."

"But, Ella, isn't everyday life more comforting?"

"Then you're not living, not stretching yourself. A life without thrills? Is it good? Is it death?" she asked.

"Well, I am not saying exactly that, Ella."

"Tell me."

"Well, you are making me look at the walls. I am keeping up in order to be able to carry on with life as a practical set of actions. If I allowed myself complete intellectual freedom, I fear I would be lost."

"Then don't fear it," she urged. "Honestly if you are convinced of this, then it will happen."

"Well, I need only a few basic 'walls'."

"Like what? You have a brilliant mind, Elias. You should set it free."

"Well, I mustn't let myself be seduced by violence, for example," he said.

"No, that's good, but why violence?"

"Violence is seductive." He wrung his hands together nervously.

"Hmm this is interesting," she commented and turned a charming smile on him.

"I intend to use walls—mental structures that help determine a stable identity."

"That means not living outside your comfort zone." She stopped and then added, "I realized that about you a long time ago."

"Well, it means you need to build your comfort zone in order to live."

She looked straight into his eyes. "Comfort zones for me are too still; they scare me. If you stay in your comfort zone, you will marvel at everything without being part of anything."

"I could move outside my zone, but then I could kill myself at some point."

"No, you wouldn't, Elias. I know you wouldn't because I know you will protect your soul from the downfall as I do. I am still the same girl who left Rio, but I like to be an observer. At first it is intimidating; then it becomes a big theatrical performance."

"Hmm I'm going to have to think about this for a while," he said.

"Truly, life threw me like this. I never intended to be a pole dancer, but now I am; I come home every night like a clown. I take off my makeup, my shoes, and with it everything else, the audience, the lights, and I am myself again playing with my daughter. I know you will be able to do it too; you were a farmer, and now you're an artist."

"Yeah, but I got depressed for a year, farming and sitting there all day long. It was horrible waiting for the day to finish so I could go back home."

"Don't underestimate yourself, and anyway who doesn't get depressed?"

"Because, Ella, I had to forget what I was."

"OK, but I'm sure you feel better now, and I'm sure you'll feel much better later."

"Yes, I do, Ella, especially when you're here next to me. You belong to me; no light, no audience, no theatre—only me."

"So you see you made it."

"Yes, I agree."

"And you still have this uncorrupted soul?"

"I will make it, Ella, when I become a famous artist."

"And guess what? You are already one, and don't use the future tense; the future is now. Believe me; I see through you."

"Not yet…not yet but I will get there…I must."

Then she looked at her watch. "I have to go now," she said.

"Do you want me to drop you?"

"No, thank you; I need some fresh air. I'll walk." Then she kissed him good-bye.

Ella and Elias met again a few days later, this time by coincidence. Ella had just dropped her daughter at friend's house when she bumped into Elias at the local market.

Elias grabbed her hand. "Come; there is a very nice café around the corner. They do the best cappuccino in the world."

"OK," Ella replied cheerfully. As they sat she went straight into a question that had been dwelling in her mind for a while.

"Do you want to have kids"?

Elias's mood changed. "No, not particularly. The main reason that people want kids is because they want them to achieve their own failed dreams and realisations. I don't want that. It's cruel."

"We all want what is best for our children."

"What we think is best doesn't mean is particularly good for them," Elias replied.

"What then? Let them choose by themselves? It doesn't make sense. My daughter is five; what should I do then? Leave her now to decide by herself? I need to guide her."

"Guiding is one thing; imposing is something else. There is a fundamental difference between tolerating another choice and ostracising and punishing if this choice doesn't suits you."

Walking back home, she realized that Elias was not for her. She had a lot of respect for him and for his achievements, but deep down she needed someone else with another mind-set. Her life to date had been dictated by others, and she knew she had to save her daughter so she would not end up the same way. She had to do something to break the circle of misery. She did not know how to tell him; she never knew how to say no to men.

Of course she had enjoyed being with him. He was so different from anyone else she ever knew. It had made her proud to be loved for once for herself and not for anything else, but now she felt two worlds separating them, and she was not as confident as she used to be.

She inhaled as deeply as she could and felt her decision was made.

-->=☐) (☐=<--

Ella decided to leave her job and drop her daughter with her mother in Rio while she made plans to move to another city without Elias and seek a better job and life. That was the plan.

Once Ella left, Elias thought for the first time that he could start a new family and that he had found this girl who with a smile had erased all his past. But things turned differently. When Elias tried to reach her desperately in Rio, she would not answer his calls and then one day she called him back.

"Hi, Elias."

"Hi," he answered, his voice low and sad. "Where have you been? I've been trying to reach you for weeks. Why didn't you answer your phone?"

"I'm sorry. I need to tell you something…look, I like you a lot and owe you everything, but I am with someone else now. He's French, and he's taking me to the Caribbean where I'm opening a fashion store."

There was heavy silence on the phone. Elias was too choked to reply.

"I just hope that whatever happens in your life, you will be happier than you've been in the past years," she said.

"How could you? Never mind," he said, and then he put the phone down.

It was as if someone had stabbed him in his heart—as if she'd ripped another strip of his flesh.

Elias immersed himself in his paintings. Ella had created the only opening of his soul, like a light coming out of darkness, and now that door was closed forever.

His thoughts were scattered for a while, and he couldn't focus on anything. He kept on asking the same question: "How could something like this have happened?" He missed her laugh, her ability to see the best in every situation, her good humour, and advice. They had been together for only a few months, but it was like a dream. The sex was not that great, but he liked to sit next to her on her bed. He never really got to know her daughter, but that was not so bad. He genuinely worried she would end up hurt as she always needed to be reassured and kept asking him how much he loved her.

Paintings became his other world where he could master colours and shapes. No one could impose on him anymore. He liked Vincenzo because he let him experience art for himself; he didn't impose his theory or methods. That's the true essence of an artist, Vincenzo told him. After a few months, his landlord refused to extend his lease, so Elias decided to move away from the town and called Vincenzo that morning.

"Hello, buddy."

"Hey, Elias, how are you? I heard you are doing well."

"Yes, thank you; but the bastard owner wants me to move, and I can't afford any higher rent, so where do you think I can go?"

"Well, let me think…Itaituba is a nice town. I have a very good friend there called Magdalena. I'll give her a phone call tomorrow. She knows several gallery owners, so probably she can find you a seller, and that way you only concentrate on your work without worrying about trying to sell your paintings."

"That sounds like a good deal. When you hear from her, tell me."

"OK; until when did the landlord give you notice?"

"I have to leave within two weeks. Apparently his daughter is moving in with her fiancé."

"OK. I'll let you know."

Two weeks later Elias moved to Itaituba. Once there he called his mother.

"Elias, how are you? I just finished praying to the Virgin Mary, and I asked her if you would call me."

"Here you are; she answered your prayer. Hello, Mum, I'm just calling to tell you that I have moved to Itaituba."

"Where is that? Are you still in Brazil?"

He laughed. "Of course, where else?"

"OK. Let me write it down. Can you spell it for me please?"

"I-t-a-i-t-u-b-a."

"Right, I have it down. How is your work? I mean what are you doing now?"

"I'm an artist and well known here."

"Good. I see. When are you coming to see me?"

"Maybe this summer, I promise."

"All right, and may God bless you, my son."

By moving far away, Elias thought he would easily forget Ella, but he couldn't, and she stayed in his mind affecting his work. At the same time, he missed Sally and tried to get in touch with her. At first she refused, she didn't return his phone calls, but gradually she opened up more.

"Sally, please don't hang up. I just need to hear your voice," he said.

Silence then. "What do you want?" she asked coldly.

"What happened? Why don't you want to talk to me?"

"Because you lied," she answered.

"How?"

"I asked Vincenzo, and he told me you'd fallen in love with Ella."

"You can't control falling in love, Sally, can you? I'm sorry."

"Why are you sorry? Keep your pity for yourself."

"You are never far from my thoughts," he said. "I've thought about what you said to me, and I can only say to you that you must clear your head of those thoughts. They're self-defeating and create a negative cycle, which causes more anguish. Find friends who are wise, kind, generous; that's where you'll find the compassion you seem to have lost.

"Like Giuseppe," she answered. "I miss him so much."

"I know; I miss him too, Sally, but I want to see you happy."

"Don't worry about me. So how is the girlfriend doing? You must be finally very happy?"

"Not quite."

"What do you mean?" she asked.

"She left me for a richer guy."

"Oh, I see. That's typical in this culture."

"Really?"

"Yes, because they're very poor. Well, look, I'm sorry; you're always welcome to come back here."

"Thank you, Sally, but all my clients are here now. I'll come back for a weekend sometime?"

"Of course. Would you paint me again?"

"I'd love to, but a different pose this time—not looking at the garden. That took ages to fix. I struggled with your profile."

A month later Elias finally could afford to visit Sally for a weekend. He took all his painting gear with him, the canvas and all of his oil tubes. She undressed and lay naked on her long white sofa.

"Am I good like this?" she said, assuming a provocative pose.

He was startled but then answered, "Yes, that's fine."

"Don't paint me the way I look."

"What do you mean?"

"I don't know. Use your own eyes," she answered.

"OK. I won't make you obvious—is that what you mean?"

"No, as you see my tits are a bit small and saggy, and I have this huge crease on my stomach. In other words make me younger."

"OK. Why we don't change the pose? Like maybe if you sit with your back to me and then tilt your face towards the right? Wouldn't that be more appealing?"

"Yes, I like that idea."

The session took three hours just to sketch her properly. "Did we finish?" she asked. "This is hurting my back."

"Yes, for the moment it's fine. I don't need you to pose anymore, and I can do the rest myself."

"But don't you need the correct light?" Looking at the sketch, she was impressed. "What else have we got to do here?"

"Add colours, shade, and highlights. I can manage; don't worry."

"Awesome," she said.

She stood up naked. Slowly and hesitantly he looked at her as she moved closer to him so he could smell her perfume.

"I miss making love to you," she said.

Elias pulled his head away slowly; the smell left his nostrils, and he started cleaning up. She felt humiliated but pretended she was not, but she still did not want him to leave.

"OK," she said, "what about a drink?"

"Yeah, a tequila please."

"A tequila? You always liked whisky."

"Yeah, but I like tequila too now," he replied defensively with a shrug.

"OK. Let me get dressed; then I'll fix your drink."

In the meantime Elias wrote in his notebook: "Maybe I should not write to you; maybe it will add malaise, but this is the way I am; I believe in human nature. Although we are culturally different, I believe we all share the same human characteristics. Acting is a metaphor for our human existence; we are all merely players that come and go, as Shakespeare said, but I believe that even on the stage of life, we are still all unpredictable. Sometimes the mask may fall. In the labyrinth of life instead of the Minotaur following us, we become the Minotaur.

Our enemy is ourselves and within. Fear is the worst plague that follows us, trying to shake our beliefs and the deepest of our convictions. Fear of the unknown is the insanity that prevents us from flying, as it binds our claws to the earth and makes us prisoners. Dreams make us alive—make us believe that the impossible can be done, that we can break from our pathetic existence to join the gods. Underneath our silence we find beauty and old habits, faith, and its rejection.

"At nineteen I wanted to taste every second of my existence. I wanted eternity and the world at my feet and to be far from the war and conflict. Travel became my own purpose. Expanding the horizon and stretching the frontiers was all to which I aspired. I conquered the world; I sat with nomads and understood what life meant to them. Apparent simplicity belied the complexity of how they perceived the world; their notion of beauty was unpredictable.

"For the first time in my life, I decided to take a train after spending the last five years on the platform, watching life's travellers going up and down. My 'journey' did not have a destination, and I felt as if I was observing my life from an external viewpoint. I observed it and never acted on it, and then after all these years I began to play my own role again. What a feeling not to be a prisoner of my soul!"

When she appeared he closed his notebook.

"What were you writing?" she asked.

"Oh, nothing. Now and again I like to write what I feel."

"Am I inside that notebook?" she smiled.

"No one is in it. It's only about me. I always lived to please people, but now I have decided to live for myself." Obviously Elias lied.

"Makes sense, Elias, and I really encourage you to do so. Don't stop for anybody; people don't see it in you, this desire for life you have in your eyes."

"Do you mean desire for death?"

"No, I didn't say that. Why are you talking about death? You are still so young, Elias."

"I don't care, and for me they are both the same. How do you know we are alive?"

"Because my beating heart tells me so."

"True; my brain and my heart tell me so then," Elias replied.

"It's a perception and misunderstanding of life. Until the brain dies, a person is not dead."

"What? Your perceptions and your conscience?"

"That's part of it, yes, Elias."

"Do you believe in God, Sally? I mean your answer is relevant after what you've suffered. Do you still think God is here?"

"I do, and I am a believer. I am a Christian. What about you?"

"No, I don't. Maybe because my mother is so devout; it's a counter reaction, but I don't. I agree with Nietzsche; he divided moralities into two types: master and slave. Slave morality gives a key definition to 'evil' and 'sin.' Good has no more substance than avoiding sin. It tells you what not to do instead of what to do. It's a nihilistic morality. Master morality gives positive content to 'good' and considers 'bad' as the absence of good. Christianity is Nietzsche's favourite example of slave morality. Nietzsche doesn't disapprove of God or Christ but treats Christianity 'as a sickness of the soul,'" Elias answered.

"You see the problem is that people expect God to intervene in our lives as a neighbour would," Sally answered. "He doesn't owe us anything. It's free will; he gives us, life, which is a blessing in itself. But people don't see it, and then when death occurs, we judge God. When my daughter died, I hated God. Of course this is normal, and even Jesus on the cross asked God 'Why did you forsake me?' but then what choice do we have at the end? He is our creator, and who knows what's on the other side. I always think it could have been worse, you know. We only lament the bad things in our lives; we are never grateful, and we should be."

"It's our existence that defines us," Elias replied. "There is no God; it's a human invention—a totem that we need for our narrative for the creation of the world and the other worlds. We come, we go, and that's it—nothing magical about it. We are organic waste; all of this earth contains the remains of people, and we walk on them every day."

⇢⊨◉ ◉⊨⇠

Elias became obsessed with writing as an antidote to his loss. Every night he would sit and write about different subjects. Once he met Vincenzo, and they both had a discussion about the importance of writing. Elias turned his mind to philosophy in an attempt to understand his condition. His writing became more defined and detailed.

The more Elias tried to save his soul from negative thoughts, the more he felt he was drowning. Sally tried to help him, but she couldn't. She once visited his studio filled with paintings of Ella—some of her face, some of her naked body—and she understood why he refused to paint her similarly and forgave him for that. He rarely left his studio, and he would go only to the local gallery owned by Diego. Magdalena, Vincenzo's friend, called him one day to invite him to a celebration of her birthday.

"I would love you to come."

"Not sure if can," he answered, "but I'll try."

"There'll be a nice crowd and a new friend of mine who's just moved to town. She knows nobody, and she's from France."

"No, please don't try to set me up with someone. I'm quite happy alone."

"I'm not, I promise."

"What shall I wear?"

"Anything; it's going to be causal."

"What are you doing? Throwing a party?"

"No; just a dinner at a restaurant. I'll send you the address later."

"OK, I'll try. When is it?"

"Next Friday."

"OK."

The next Friday Elias felt strangely joyful. He dressed himself and headed towards the restaurant. Once introduced to everybody, he sat on the edge of the table. His mood changed as he stared at the people, their mouths opening and closing; he was studying their gestures and their expressions when one of the girls looked at him.

"Do you agree with me?"

He looked surprised and looked at her. "Sorry, you lost me," he said, and then after a silence, "Oh…I agree with all of it."

They both laughed. He was bored. What was he doing with these strange people?

"So what do you do?" the girl asked.

"I'm an artist," he replied.

"Oh, it's you! Magdalena always talks about you. You're the guy from Lebanon, no?"

"Yes, I am."

"How is the situation there now?"

"I don't know. I don't follow politics."

"I heard it was ugly. That's why you left I guess—the car bombs, I mean, it sounds horrible. The massacre they w…"

"I beg your pardon, but where is the toilet here?" Elias interrupted her.

"Oh, just there—on your right."

Elias headed to the toilet, and once there he felt like throwing up in the cubicle. Why on earth did people always want to intrude in his life? He couldn't stand it and decided to leave. Once out of the toilet, he headed to his table to retrieve his cigarettes when he saw Magdalena coming towards him with a girl walking behind her.

"Elias," she called.

"Yes," he turned.

Chapter 14

MARY HELPED LAURA as much as she could, but she also needed some privacy in her flat. Not wanting to be a burden, Laura went to the Brazilian embassy and asked for a work visa.

"Because Elias is there," said Mary. "Are you mad, Laura? Going like this with a young child just to follow your heart?"

"It's unfinished business; I need to know," she said, staring at her friend.

"To know what? The guy left, never looked at you twice, and he didn't even say good-bye."

"Why do you need constantly to remind me about bad things?"

"Because I'm your friend, and I love you. I'm not entirely sure what the outcome will be; will he, for instance, be happy to see you? How do you know if he's still single and not married?"

"I love you too, but I need you to understand, and I need some closure. I don't know, but his mother would probably have told you on the phone if he was married."

"She doesn't know anything about him, poor woman; he's not close to her at all. He barely talks to her. Anyway you are very stubborn, and you will end up doing what you want."

"Exactly, because, Mary, we have only one life, and I want to follow my dream so I won't regret it one day. I already lost half of my life in wrong decisions, and this time I want to do the right thing."

"I'm not sure he is the right thing, that's all. When are you leaving?"

"As soon as they authorize a visa for me."

"You can stay here, you know."

"I know, but you need some privacy too, and I can't just stay forever. We've been here for almost five months."

"True; I won't lie to you."

"Please, Mary, could you do me a favour and call his mother?"

"Again? To say what?"

"I want to know if she knows where he lives."

"OK; let's try now." Mary picked up the phone and dialled the number that Laura showed her.

"Hello, Tante, how are you? Sorry to bother you again; it's Mary here. Do you remember I called you some time ago?"

Silence.

"OK. I'm just…err…travelling to Brazil for my holidays. Do you know by chance where Elias lives now?" Mary looked from the phone to Laura and back to the phone.

"Ah, OK; what's the name of the town again in the state of Para? Itaituba? OK, thank you very much, and what does he do? He is what…a painter? Do you mean an artist? Ah, OK, sure, great! Thank you again."

"So," Laura said excitedly. "Itaituba? Very funny name—Itaituba, Itaituba," repeating the word like a child; her brain throbbed from the excess of details and images. She wanted suddenly and desperately to be with him, to hug him, and to talk to him about their shared and common past.

"Let's look at it on the computer," she said, so they both looked.

"Oh, gosh! It's in the middle of nowhere," Mary said.

"Well, at least that way he's mine, and nobody will have him."

"I can't believe my eyes and ears that you'll go to the end of the world for this man, Laura! At least let's track him down so you can call him and have a feel of the situation and know whether he will want to see you or not. And then where are you going to work there? You know I don't know if you are aware that this is a change in career, a lifestyle, even for your daughter's education. You have to give it a great deal of thought."

"Look, let's throw a party, and we'll invite Olivier and his Brazilian girl-friend, and I'll ask her if she knows someone there where I can work. She owes me that after stealing my boyfriend; don't you think so?"

After five weeks Laura was granted a visa. Mary threw a big party for her friend, which a lot of people from work attended. That morning Laura busied herself with cooking mini-pizzas in the oven and making the sauce for the vegetables. Once the Latino music started kicking in, the guests arrived.

The drink flowed, music played, and after it all Laura felt exhausted. Olivier didn't show up, so his girlfriend must have made a scene or a fuss, or he didn't even care if Laura was staying or leaving. Mary promised she'd ask her at work tomorrow.

The next day Mary came in excited.

"OK, you are lucky. She knows someone who knows most of the people of the town, and apparently she can find you a job. This lady is in the art business, so maybe you can work in a gallery? Who knows! But aren't you worried that his mum will tell him that there is this Lebanese girl inquiring about him?"

"Yes, she might." Laura suddenly felt terrified. "You're absolutely right but hopefully not."

"Aren't you going to tell Louis and your parents?"

"I'll call my mum tomorrow. I won't tell them now or at least maybe only my mum. When I think how long it took my father to let me leave Beirut, it's going to be hell for him to let me leave France."

"But you're not a child anymore, Laura; you're a grown woman. Nobody should interfere with your decision."

"I know, but I have a very difficult father," Laura muttered rubbing her hands over her face.

"Well, set up boundaries—you should. Then tell your mum, and she'll get him to agree. For Louis you can say you're going for a long vacation or something."

Laura nodded. "This could work," she said and added, "It's going to be wonderful I'm sure."

"OK," Mary yawned. "I have to sleep. Call me tomorrow when you've spoken to your parents."

"Yes. Goodnight."

Laura called her mother, thinking of a reasonable excuse for her travel.

"So you're travelling? With your daughter I hope."

"Of course, Mum, I won't leave her, but don't tell Dad."

"No, I won't tell him, but who you are going to see there?"

"Elias."

"Who?"

"Elias; do you remember?"

"That idiot? Why on earth are you bothering yourself with a guy like that?"

"There is no particular reason. I just want a change of scenery. I'm stuck here, and nobody will look at me as I have a daughter now."

"You always had your father's stubbornness. What can I say? When will you be leaving?"

"Less than a month. I need to sort myself out first."

"Well, when you get there, call me. Where will you work?"

"I'll work in an art gallery."

"Don't you need some knowledge of art?"

"Yes, that's why I'm enrolling in this intensive course in how to sell art. The local council runs it, and they also teach you how to paint."

"Oh, I see. Well, take care of yourself, and don't forget to call me."

"I will; love you. Bye."

The next day Laura enrolled in the course and spent the remaining few weeks taking notes from the teacher and even made a huge effort to learn how to mix colours properly and how to paint on canvas. It was not easy for her as most of the students were professional artists attending the course just to get the diploma. Mary encouraged her to visit Lebanon just before leaving for Brazil as it was a shorter flight from Paris, and who knew when she would be able to get back in the future? After the course had finished, Laura packed and went to Lebanon.

Her father was waiting for her at the airport, very upset in his usual way, thought Laura. He helped her and her daughter into the car and then drove them to the family home, where her mother greeted them with a big smile.

"Long time no see," her mother said.

"Hello, Mum, nice to see you," she said, and then she murmured, "Why is Dad always in a bad mood?"

"He is not in a bad mood; he is just upset that you divorced."

"Did you tell him about Brazil? I hope not."

"No, I haven't told him yet."

"OK, so don't," Laura said in her mother's ear.

"How long are you staying here with us?" her father asked.

"Only a few days, Dad." She couldn't stay longer—everything around her was a reminder of a sad and lost life.

The next day Laura walked around the streets of her little town and felt a great happiness. A lot had happened since she left. She wanted to see Philippe from the embassy, but she didn't know what to say. She missed him somehow; he was really a very nice guy. She hailed a cab and asked him to drop her at the French Consulate where she asked the security staff where she could find him.

"He doesn't work here anymore; he left a year ago and went back to France," one of the guards told her.

"To France?"

"Oh, I don't know, to be honest, but he left."

"OK; thank you for your time," she said in a disappointed voice.

Laura walked home through the bustling traffic, dust, and heat, hearing the usual occasional compliments from local workers. She felt the sun's strong heat on her head and enjoyed it. She liked dirty cities and the sounds of children playing in the background. She couldn't deal with clean cities; she found them harsh and lonely—they had no soul. She loved Lebanon, but like Gibran Khalil Gibran, her favourite writer, she had her own Lebanon that was pure and uncorrupted.

This was the only place in the world where she could be herself and feel happy in a pure suspended state. As she headed home, Laura dug back in her memories. The streets for her were heavily charged with nostalgia; every corner told a story of love or death. The war had passed, but signs of it remained. Bullet holes and mortar-damaged buildings could be seen everywhere, and photos of young men labelled "Martyr" still hung on church walls. She stopped and stared at each one of them, in case she recognized them. A war had scattered the nation; most of her family were dispersed to the four corners of this world, and yet you could see couples bound together, hugging and giving lingering kisses. They were dark figures moving around the corners of these streets. This was her Lebanon—death could not win; people still had life in their veins. War was a theatre—a stage for a play about the brevity of human glory or human failure, and words were sometimes too clumsy to describe it. She looked at one couple embracing and said, "Is it the best place to do this?"

They stopped kissing and turned surprised towards her. He was a huge corpulent man, wearing a stained formal suit with no tie and a shirt opened halfway down his chest. He shrugged. "It's the way I like it," he said. "It's more exciting," and with a throaty, self-satisfied voice, he said, "Do you want me to kiss you too?" and he smiled. Laura gazed at him. "Ah," she said, "that's charming, but no, thank you."

Then the girl dragged her boyfriend away, looking at Laura, fear in her eyes but with her lips full and sensual.

So Laura continued walking and wishing Elias was there with her and realizing how convention forced people into ridiculous behaviour.

Then she passed near the café where she used to meet Philippe. She wanted to go inside for an iced tea. The tablecloth was the same and even the waiter. She looked at him in case he remembered her, but he looked at her blankly.

"What can I do for you?" he asked. His hair looked wavy, unwashed, and uncombed over his sweaty forehead.

"Could I have an iced tea with lemon please?"

"We don't have that, I am afraid."

"You took it off the menu? I always had that here."

"Ah, but we changed management, so the menu changed too."

"I see; so I'll take a hot tea instead."

"English breakfast?"

"Thanks, that will do," she said and then chose the same seat where she used to sit with Philippe.

"Excuse me," she followed the waiter. "Have you seen Philippe lately? He used to work at the French consulate."

"No, I saw him briefly with his girlfriend, about a year ago."

"His girlfriend," she muttered.

"Yes, the blond girl, but I think they left for the US."

"Both?" she asked arching her eyebrows wryly.

"I think they got married and left."

"Oh, I see. Thank you very much."

"You're welcome. I'll bring your tea shortly."

Laura was devastated. She tried to calm herself with a sip of tea, but she choked on it instead. After coughing several times, she started crying. She shook her head. He must be mistaken, she thought, feeling something twist in her gut; I mean probably he confused him with another Frenchman. How does he know he is the same guy? Philippe doesn't introduce himself everywhere with 'Hey, I'm Philippe. I work at the consulate!' She quickly paid and left. She was surprised. He wasn't lying after all when he said he was willing to leave his wife. Oh well, this is all destined to happen. Dad always said nobody takes anything from you, Laura; you will only have what is destined for you, she thought. Then she felt better.

When she finally arrived home, she was depressed. Her mother greeted her with an account of her day with Leila who she said was the most intelligent little girl in the world.

"Interesting," said Laura listening to her mother.

"I thought you only went for a short walk, yet you disappeared for almost three hours. She was crying waiting for you."

Laura gasped, speechless for a moment, and then said, "God, what is it? I'm not nineteen years old."

Her father appeared from the door of his room.

"No, you're not nineteen, but when you're in my house, you respect my rules. At least you should have the decency to call us; we were worried as hell."

"Sorry, Dad I didn't take my phone with me, and the SIM is French. If I call you, it will cost me a fortune."

"So buy yourself a Lebanese SIM."

"I'm only here for few days. Why should I?"

"Well, think why. You're a mother, and we should be able to reach you if your daughter has a problem."

"OK. I'll sort it out," Laura said. "Now can I go and eat?"

After dinner Laura thought it was time for her to go back to France; no need to stay any longer. She would find an excuse to leave after tomorrow instead of staying another four days. The next day she confronted her parents.

"I got a phone call and have to go back to Paris for an urgent matter with Louis," her voice sounded tense.

"Why?" said her father. He wiped his mouth, stood up, and lurched from the table. "After leaving the poor guy who did everything for you, you are now going to rescue him?" Laura felt as if she'd been bathed in ice. "I'm not going to rescue him; I have to talk to him."

"So when are you leaving?"

"Tomorrow. There's a flight at nine. I'll take that."

Her mother was devastated, and Laura felt a deep sadness at leaving her parents, especially as she knew that her father had had a heart attack last summer. She reached out to her mother and grabbed her hand and kissed it.

"I love you, Mum, but this is not for me. Too many memories here. I need to escape and go back."

"What the hell do you think you are doing, Laura? Escaping from here to go to another problem?"

Laura tensed and then relaxed. "You're always so negative; you have to give me the benefit of the doubt sometimes."

"Now this is you bullshitting. No need for that you know; I'm on your side, but he's the wrong guy for you, Laura. He's selfish, and you never mattered to him. He didn't even come home for his father's funeral."

"It's not for us to judge; you don't know his situation."

"Enough of making excuses for people. You always want to see the bright side of every individual but it doesn't work like that. Ninety-nine per cent of people are bad and not genuine."

"What does that leave me with, Mum?"

"I don't know. Just look after yourself and your daughter, darling."

Laura spent her last day with her parents, sitting at home, listening to her father talking about everything from politics to religion and playing chess with him, his favourite game. A sudden loud bang made her gasp and sit up. "What's that?" she shouted nervously.

"Nothing," said her father. "Don't worry; the days of bombs are behind us. It was probably a firework." She sank back in her chair and took a deep breath. "Too many memories of bad times," she said. With shaking hands her father poured two glasses of whisky. He sipped his gratefully and then looked at her. "In eight years I'll be gone—write it down," he said; his eyes suddenly looked wild and desperate.

"What do you mean by 'gone'?"

"I mean dead, Laura."

She drank her whisky. The fiery burn warmed her throat, and she looked at him doubtfully. "You've been going at this stuff a bit too seriously, Dad. Nobody knows the hour of their death, and you're talking eight years."

"I ain't nobody; I'm God," he said and then he laughed.

She felt a great sadness because deep inside her she knew she would not be there at that moment. "I love you, Dad," she said and kissed him. "I'm sure you will bury me first."

"Don't say that; I'll be here at the wedding of your daughter," he said sadly and smiled. "When will you come back to see us?"

"I'll be back before you even know."

He pulled himself together with a visible effort. "I love you, Laura." He gave her a tight hug. "You're a very good person."

"So don't judge me, Dad."

There was a glint in his eyes, which meant he refuted her words, but it was not the time or the place to rehash another argument.

"Why do you keep on whispering to your mother then?"

"I'm not."

"Yes, you are; I'm sure you're hiding something. Don't take me for a fool."

"No, it's just that I was thinking of going to Brazil to try my luck there."

"Why Brazil? Why so far?"

"I can't find a proper job in Paris, and Louis is not helping much." There was tightness in her throat. Everybody seemed to think that her choice was odd, and she was the only one who was positive about it.

"Just be careful. It's too far, and it's riddled with poverty, so how you're going to find a job there I have no idea."

She could understand her father's gentle concern and decided not to discuss it further. Her mother interrupted them with a bowl of fresh fruit.

"Do you want me to peel you an apple, Laura?"

"Please, Mum," she said and then excused herself and disappeared into her daughter's bedroom. Her parents sat in silence; they looked helpless and old. With a sigh her mother proposed to make two Nescafés while her father gazed into the void and nodded.

⊷▸▰◉ ◉▰◂⊶

The next day her parents were up, and the taxi was waiting already to take her to the airport. She hugged both of them and then went down the stairs in case a power cut stopped the lift and got into the taxi. In the departure lounge, she looked at her daughter with a strained smile and hugged her as they waited to board the plane.

"We have lots of adventures waiting for us," she said. "But don't tell Daddy. It's our little secret."

But Leila went on playing with her Barbie.

Landing in Paris Charles de Gaulle was a relief after a bumpy journey, and after retrieving her luggage she called Mary.

"Hey, I'm here," she said over the phone.

"Already?" asked Mary.

"Yes, I couldn't stay any longer; besides the situation sucks."

"Yes, I heard that. OK, great; I'll see you tonight."

It took Laura eleven years to leave Paris for Brazil, where her best friend had found her a job in a gallery in Itituba. The day she announced to Leila they were going to Brazil, the little girl with her messy blond curls and wide eyes started crying.

"Why the tears?" Laura asked, putting her book aside. "We are not going forever; don't worry—you will see Daddy again. Remember you will spend every summer with him."

"You are not nice to Daddy. I know we are not coming back," Leila said simply and firmly.

Laura bent down and gave her a clumsy kiss on her cheeks and said jokingly, "You smell nicer than I expected." Then she sat in silence, sadness lurking in her eyes. "And if Elias was in love with someone else?" this idea invaded her early happy thoughts and enthusiasm. Then she stood up placid and calm as if nothing had happened at all.

On the console in front of Mary's room sat her wedding photograph, a bittersweet picture. Laura held it for a moment; she felt a bit of nostalgia but at the same time a sense of relief that it had ended. It had been a very difficult marriage, and she was aware that her daughter might have suffered a lot.

The marriage had lasted only six years. Even that was too long. She could not stand him anymore. He was an immature, unsuccessful lover, a graceless communicator, and unable to cope with life. She had been very unhappy, and some of her friends told her to seal off this part of her past and bury it, but she needed to talk about it.

All other men she met felt that they had to satisfy her in some way, and they were extremely careful and mindful of her having an orgasm, but sometimes even that was not enough. It was what she wanted, and she thought of it as white gold but the more she ran after it the more it escaped her. Even when she had it, she rejected it and looked for another man.

She was continuously looking for a new beginning. Once a man whom she had met on her first holiday alone with her daughter asked her about her story. Yes, absolutely, she answered and told him about her life, but he continually asked more and more questions, as if he didn't believe her. Why then did everyone keep on asking her the same question? She felt empty most of the time.

⇥═◉ ◉═⇤

Laura spent the last few days packing for Brazil. Her flight was Sunday morning on June 18, 1996. She was terrified, but she had to start a new life, and she was adamant that this move could bring her a life-changing opportunity, and if she did not take it now, it would be too late. Maybe finally she could start a new life with Elias; she was still young and could still have children. On Friday morning she boarded the flight to Rio de Janeiro; it was the last countdown. When the plane finally landed, Laura firmly took her daughter's hand and dragged their luggage behind her. Then she went to find the internal flight to Para.

She had a fleeting moment of panic when she glanced at the poor people hanging around at the airport. Then she passed a mirror, and she saw fine lines in her face and some grooves fanning out from the edge of her eyes. Startled by this vision of herself, she turned and looked away. "I have to be happy, and I have to succeed whatever the cost is. I am going to work in this gallery," she muttered.

Chapter 15

LAURA WORE HER best outfit—a red silk dress with nothing underneath, which clung to her figure outlining her firm high breasts. She entered through wide doors engraved with the name of the gallery. Inside were white leather chairs and two windows facing the southeast that allowed natural light to fill the oval space. A middle-aged man was sitting on the stairs; his hair stood on end, and his shirt was only half tucked in. Diego, the gallery owner, approached her with a big smile.

"Hi, so are you, Laura?"

"Yes."

"Magdalena told me you studied art in France?"

"I did for three years."

"Are you sure you want to work here? It means long hours, you know. And far from downtown. You will also have a target to reach every month in order to get a bonus on top of your salary."

"OK," she said. "I know; I've rented a small apartment down the road."

"OK," he said and dug into his pocket and brought out a handful of paper money. "Take this; it will help you with expenses. Magdalena spoke highly of you. I'll hire you because of your languages too."

"Thank you."

She signed her contract, folded it, and gave it to him. Now in Brazil, she knew deep inside her that she would meet Elias again.

It was early in the morning when the door rang. The postman handed her a beautiful silk paper decorated with a red handmade flower. When she unfolded it, a note invited her to a birthday party in a week's time at the Ruiz restaurant a half an hour ride from her small flat.

It was Magdalena's thirtieth birthday. Magdalena was a rich friend of Mary. They met in Paris some years ago. She was a beautiful girl with long brown hair and green almond eyes; a gentle soul, the kind that Laura felt relaxed with. Magdalena felt lonely, but Laura knew they would be good friends in this remote small town, so she smiled as she read the invitation. Finally she would meet people here.

The day of the birthday party she wore her most beautiful dress. She felt a bit apprehensive but happy. She decided to walk to the lovely locally owned café in her high heels. It took her time to find it as the number was not clearly displayed, but after asking many people she managed to enter a double door with a round black aluminium handle. Beyond the door a long corridor ended in a thick red velvet curtain. The receptionist met her behind the curtain and took her to her table. She was among the first to arrive; then Magdalena appeared very elegant with a fashionable jacket and handmade skirt. Her flowing hair had curls, and she looked radiant. Magdalena steered her gently from the door and back to the guest table and introduced her to the few people sitting there. Then she went with her to the end of the table and playfully introduced her to a man.

"And now you've seen the whole face of the moon," she said.

At the sound of Magdalena's voice, Elias stood up, and it took him a few seconds to recognize Laura. For a moment her beauty and the transformation from a girl to a fully grown woman stunned him. The Gods had woven the thread of destiny, and he smiled.

Laura found it difficult to get her head around the fact that he was there in front of her.

"Hey, how are you? Long time no see," he said. "So you know Magdalena?"

"Oh yes, I knew her in France."

"France? That is a long way to come for a dinner," he laughed.

"Oh no, I've moved here now."

"Why?"

"Euh…just divorced…"

"Oh dear; sorry to hear that."

"And you?"

"What about me?"

"Are you married?"

"Marriage is not for me."

Laura preferred fewer things and more of his presence. She knew instantly that he was the love of her life. He had changed—still very handsome, tall, intense, and restless. She tried to breathe deeply to calm her pounding heart; she bit her lip. She really wanted to be alone with him.

"So what are you doing here? Working?"

"Yes. I work at the art gallery."

"With Diego?"

"Yes. Do you know him?"

"Yes, I occasionally sell my paintings there."

"Ah, so you are a painter then."

"Yes…you seem surprised."

"Oh no." She laughed at the ludicrous thought that he was an artist now. She dithered, undecided over whether to go sit somewhere else or to stay next to him. From his body language, he wasn't very keen on anything, with his floppy hair and the white teeth he was flashing at Magdalena. Then suddenly he left Laura and walked through the revolving doors, squeezing both his hands tightly; then he came back and pulled her towards him in a brotherly bear hug of an embrace.

She felt tearful; she softly whispered in his ear, "I missed you so much. I really would love to see you again."

After the party, she watched him walking and waving as he climbed inside the car, but as it pulled away, the smile on her face slowly slid away. His words echoed in her mind.

"Yes, of course, I would be happy to take you out next week; take my number from Magdalena and call me."

Once in her bed, she felt happy, extremely happy, as for once life was fair to her. No big fuss here; he was in front of her. What a coincidence. She touched his business card and kissed it, put it on the table near her bed, and slept. She recalled those first magical moments we all dream about—a touch, a kiss. She started imagining being his wife with two kids and a house; her imagination ran wild. I am a very sad person, Laura thought.

⊷▭◉ ◉▭⊶

It was good to meet someone she knew, especially in front of her friends. She pretended to have a common history, with common friends; for once she was with people she had known for a long time. She wanted to be attached to him; she wanted to be in love. For once finally someone understood her, someone who lived in the same world as her.

She called him the next day, and they set up a dinner in a local *asado* for the following week. He arrived almost an hour late, pulling an apologetic face when he showed up.

"Sorry; I wanted to be earlier, but I couldn't. I had a last minute client."

"It's fine," she replied.

He seemed unsettled for the rest of the dinner, and the atmosphere was definitely not romantic. He was very keen on talking about his past, and she allowed him to.

They talked for hours about Mounir and their childhood memories—their silly mischief like throwing stones on the ducks or fireworks on old people. Nobody existed anymore for her in the noisy restaurant; she was in her own silent world. Words flowed as the wine was poured into their glasses, and her head was spinning and turning like a Turkish dervish. They talked and remembered the war. Then he talked about his last exhibition and how some philosophers reacted to his theme, "Never close your eyes," and how the debate became intense with one of the philosophers. His view of the world as catastrophic matched some modern philosophy. She argued that catastrophe came to an end, but he disagreed. Catastrophe was unpredictable, he said. You have to live the future in order to know whether your actions were catastrophic. Jokingly, he said that probably their encounter was catastrophic; then he went on talking about the passionate love affair he had with a Brazilian stripper a few years back and how she would always be the love of his life. She looked at his expressions and his blue eyes. He had lost weight, and his face was so thin. Love was never meant to be such a beautiful feeling. Anyway she never believed in love, but she dreamt about being his stripper turning around this metal pole dancing and making love to him. She thought, How did it feel to have men looking at her and dreaming of touching her while in reality she wanted only one man, the one staring at her in the corner? Then she tried to go inside the stripper's head and eyes; she tried to imagine how he would be with her. What did she think of him? Why did she leave him? He gave her everything, his life, his time.

He left his world for her. But who knows why. People have their reasons—generally only one, because when love dies, it is replaced with excuses. People need excuses and explanations for why love comes and goes suddenly. That was a universal secret. Why do we love one or two people in a whole life? Some call it chemistry, some sexuality, desire, and obsession. The edge—once it is reached, everything goes back to calm, no big deal; reason takes over. This is where people start thinking, and love ceases to be. She wondered why he needed to tell her about this old love. It was two years ago, and he is still thinking about it, dreaming about her—she was still on his mind.

"Why did you persist with her?"

"With whom?"

"Sorry, I meant the stripper."

"Ah, I thought I would give it a go—that I finally found the love of my life, and if it didn't work, I would leave. The realisation that I could never reach this degree of love made me leave."

She nodded frantically, slightly baffled, and then sighed and looked away. Actually, she thought he truly loved her, but he never loved me that way. Then she gasped and reeled backwards with her chair.

"Are you OK?" he asked. "You seem to be in agony."

"Oh yes," she said, straightening her chair. "I was just wondering, were you happy with her...I mean you must have adored her?"

"Pretty much." The muffled beat of music interrupted him then he added, "Honestly, I think I am fine now. I really don't need to go to those places anymore."

"What do you mean?"

"I meant all this passion and love stuff."

She wished she could walk away. She thought, did I not know that it would be like this? She was not sure if he was directing these thoughts towards her; her mind was racing. Then she calmed herself. Life is an illusion; after seeing him the first time she realized that he was secretive, and she could not get inside him. Does this matter, she thought? Yes, years ago it would have been a problem, but now who cares? She preferred it that way; keeping a wall between them was not so bad, and she did not want him to read her either. Openness is boring, effortless; what keeps a couple together was always a question, and she was full of questions. The only problem was that each time they saw each other, she thought things were perfectly fine as neither of them wanted to ask the awkward questions; they both pretended that things were great or wanted to believe it, but then when they parted, questions raced in her head, so she wished she could run back and ask him.

→⊨● ●⊨←

At the sound of the doorbell, Laura skipped down the stairs towards the main door, but in her hurry she slammed into Elias.

"Oh sorry," she said taken aback. Then, recovering, she said, "What a nice surprise!"

He had come to the gallery with one of his oil paintings, a woman sitting on a rock looking at a landscape.

"What do you think?" he asked.

He stood waiting politely, but the expression on his face was stoic when he saw her upturned lips.

"I'm intrigued, that's all," she said and waited for him to say something, but he remained silent. Her feet felt stuck to the floor, she didn't know what to say.

"Do you know this woman?" she asked.

"How is that relevant? I don't always understand your questions."

"Sorry, I mean she looks familiar."

"To you or to me? How could she look familiar to you if we haven't seen each other for a long time?"

His jaw tightened, and he turned his back to her.

"Sorry; I sound stupid; I was just trying to make conversation."

This is so humiliating, she thought, trying to breathe normally.

She had never questioned the certainty that they would be together one day before now, but from the way he spoke to her, she began to doubt his intentions towards her. He was clearly keeping something from her. She triggered a past that he had thought buried forever. Then he stroked her hair and kissed the top of her head, and she felt guilty about her earlier thoughts.

"No, you don't know her; she used to be my uncle's big love. She came to visit us, and I drew her looking at the garden."

"I am sorry. I just imagined you with a different style, that's all…more masculine perhaps. The way you've drawn her is as you were both in love."

The sight of him standing there calmly brought tears to her eyes; she turned away and stomped upstairs to the office.

Elias followed her, his face tense; his mind worked at something to say, but he just could not utter a word. He drew a blank—not one word of comfort came to him. He realized Laura was too young and innocent for him. She wanted him to protect her, yet she understood him better than anyone he had ever met in his life, which was why he had to run away from her.

He stared at his pale image reflected in a piece of art mixed with stained glass, a huge painting, leaning on the wall. He hesitated a moment and then said, "True, I loved this woman too; does it show so much from my painting?"

Suddenly she was crying uncontrollably, her head buried in her hands; she seemed devastated.

"Why? Why did you love her?" she blurted through the tears.

"Laura, I wish I had an answer for you, but I don't. I felt safe with her. She transformed me physically and mentally. When I met her, she was a broken woman; she had just lost her daughter. She needed love, and I needed to give love." He paused and then looked at his surroundings; the stucco was peeling away in some places.

"The whole affair was overwhelming…"

"Do you still see her? Do you still love her?" she said between gasps.

"Oh, please, Laura."

"You lied to me; you told me you only loved your Brazilian stripper."

"It takes time, Laura, to adjust from a dark room to bright lights."

"What is your dark room? Even in a dark room, shafts of light could stream through."

He continued looking at the stained glass, wondering what the artist had meant; then he suddenly saw a multitude of shafts of light above his head and almost everywhere in the room.

"What do you really know about darkness, Laura? You had a very sheltered childhood."

She crossed her legs to keep them from shaking and then gulped. He was mocking her with blinding arrogance.

"So it is about that then…it is about our childhood. So yours allows you to do whatever you want in the name of your suffering, and mine, as it was sheltered, condemns me to a life of boredom. Is this is how you see it?"

He tossed a coin in the air and then caught it with his hand, and his gaze fell upon her.

"I believe you came into my life for a reason," he said. "Everything in my life was staid and normal before you showed up. I thought I escaped my life unscathed. I thought I would fool everybody, that I could create a character unlike my real self. I needed to reinvent myself, and I managed here to be an artist in a small lost village at the edge of nowhere as you described it to me the first night I met you. And here you are appearing in my life to take me back to places I don't want to be."

His eyes were rimmed red. She wanted to scream that she loved him above the universe and that she had failed in her marriage because she could not forget him for one minute. She wanted to comfort him, reassure him; her thoughts were pulsing like crashing waves. Her head was spinning; she felt she was suffocating. She forced herself to think about other things as a ball of dread grew in her stomach. Then she panicked at the thought that she had left everything behind—a kind of stable life, just to be here with him. She suddenly realized that he was slipping from her hands, and the most important thing wasn't Sally or the Brazilian stripper. It was him.

"Please can you kiss me. I feel I will collapse. I need you to rescue me from my darkness too. Can you hold me with your strong hands so I don't collapse?" All the time she was talking to him, tears were streaming down her face.

He jumped back at the force of her words. He felt that she was demanding too much, too quickly, that he wasn't ready. The image of her on the stairs in Lebanon where she was waiting to be kissed and comforted came back to him as a vivid image; it pierced him. The few seconds were interminable; he felt he was back in a dark room with no way out.

His expression gave nothing away; he just stood up and left. She waited until she heard the bell and then wiped her tears and went downstairs. The painting was gone.

She thought again about the banality of love—why was it important? What made it special? She concluded she could live without it. Love is a death—when we make love, we die to be reborn again. We attain the peak of our being, and beyond it there is silence, but this time his silence was different. She looked thoughtfully at the ceiling; her eyes were pinned to it, and looking at a series of small holes she found there, she started to count them. Her mouth was dry. She was surrounded by silence. Silence was the greatest sound of all, as silence can get almost to the soul. Silence is a sacred link between life and God; silence was something she had mastered from the age of eight, and in the house where she grew up, she needed to build a wall between her and the world. She needed to isolate herself from the world of madness—the madness of war. Wars are different and independent entities, and nobody can emulate them. Wars are the instances where humanity left, where personal grudges are resolved, where all noble feelings are just blown away. Personal justice replaced law. How can we mention justice when war takes everything from you? Who is the victim? The killer or the killed? She had known eleven years of war, and nobody cared. Had she never lived it, she would have been a different girl—maybe like this stripper, dancing her life away. She was a random page in a book where none of the pages knew to which book they belonged, nor which genre, a comedy, or a tragedy, which theme, death or life, which end or which beginning. When she got married, she started to see a therapist, and she remembered in Paris, he told her once that she should not look at her life as different chapters but rather a whole book. She did not believe in that—she only believed in metamorphosis or stages of evolution that one self ends up with many selves, or a whole self with many layers, as a room full of furniture where each one can be placed in a different position without impacting the layout of the room.

Elias had told her about never closing her eyes and about realising how walls appear and separate and divide people, creating an everlasting prison. He asked her about her wall. His wall was religion, he said, standing between him and paradise. She couldn't answer him. Walls suddenly became impenetrable, she thought, and far from being spiritual, they were physical. She wondered why people always made her feel as if she was the only one erecting walls.

After a silence of ten days, Elias had sent her a message three days ago telling her that he thought of her as a light, an image in a transparent mirror with no background, that he couldn't keep her in his mind. This was a thick wall, but why did he need to tell her that? Now she was here waiting for him, but maybe he had decided to leave his wall in place? She thought finally that she had broken it and gone through. She felt very proud; she'd danced in the street and laughed until a man passing by looked at her as if she was crazy. Now she realized that life had fooled her again. Just as when she was eight and love and all good things were only fireflies in the garden, a myth, a sort of mirage in the desert and an awakening. The past again. Elias told her that it should be a steppingstone for the future, but was it really? Her life was full of memories of her past, and if she left them behind, she wouldn't know where to go.

As a painter Elias lived in two parallel words, the real one, which he considered uninteresting and predictable, and his dream world, which was unpredictable, but then everything that happens in life is unpredictable, he reasoned. He had tried to teach her to put the past behind, but if she took it with her in the unpredictable world, what would happen? Imagination and past go together—how can you imagine a world if you do not have a past that you can borrow from, Laura claimed.

He wrote short stories and then posted them to himself so that each morning he drank a cup of coffee while reading the newly arrived story, so the past story became a present one. Laura could not move out of the past; she was attached to it like how that stripper was linked by a chain to the metal pole. Laura was bound to her memories; she couldn't dance freely. She wished she could leave the audience, the stage, and run down the stairs out into the street. Even there, when she looked at bits of trash, every abandoned bottle or piece of garbage had a story. Who had left it there, and why?

→—=◉ ◉=—←

Behind the grey sky, there was a kind of beauty, and she felt alive with the cold breeze touching her body. Two days before Valentine's Day, Laura sat at an outdoor café table, sipping ginger tea, hoping for a phone call, a card, or flowers. She went to the flower shop nearby, which was festooned with garlands of red paper flowers to tempt romantic customers. Among the cards with their messages of love, one of them caught her eye. "Please be my Valentine," it read. This sweet, tender message made her wish Elias was less cold. She could take the cold breeze, but she struggled to accept a cold heart. It was too hard for her to cope with after what she'd lived through during the war. She thought that God had given her fair share of hardship and now she could have a fulfilled, calm life.

She picked up her phone and called Elias. They hit it off really quickly although she did the talking. She could tell he liked that, and he sounded in a good mood responding each time she said something. He seemed to agree for the first time that he was interested in things that were important for her—such as her plans for staying in Itituba and how she could improve her life with better work and more experience in art. But then the conversation lagged as she ran out of things to talk about, and she had to fill it with banalities about her daughter's school and the play she was rehearsing. Then there was silence. He ended the conversation and said he had work to do and hung up.

After a week she started e-mailing him, but got no answer, until she called him to say she was worried about his silence and thought something had happened to him. Elias was bemused by her call. Laura felt awkward and silly, so she just laughed nervously and apologized. She explained her behaviour was an effect of the war and hung up. The silence grew between them, and each time she saw him, she would remind him of it.

She decided that he finally saw in her what he had been looking for all his life, especially as he told her he needed a woman with whom he could discuss philosophy. However, it turned out he was only interested in explaining his views on the world and wouldn't listen to her, just continuing with his own discourse whenever she attempted any discussion. Laura soon realized he only needed someone to listen to him. She began to see her life as a charade—a life lived by a proxy and not by her.

What am I doing wrong? Why do they all feel the same about me? She kept on repeating to herself. She never loved and was loved at the same time. It was always the same story of two passing trains in different directions. She was a tormented soul; her never-ending quest for peace continued years after the war.

Once Elias asked her what was her worst nightmare. For her, her whole life seemed to be a bad dream: she found it hard living far from home and trying to adapt to a different culture and society. She explained how culture was an important part of her self-image and the dubious authenticity of the society that surrounded her had blighted her chances of happiness. Here principles and values had changed, creating a chaos that perpetuated her anxiety. Maybe her worst nightmare was to die here alone and not be able to reach home.

What was his worst nightmare? she had asked Elias, and he had replied, "To go back home!"

She felt she had ventured into a difficult territory. Suspicious, she asked, "You must be kidding me; why? You will never find a better life than in your own country; you fought for it, so how can you be so negative about it?"

He had scorned her last comments.

"I didn't fight for it...I thought initially I did, but it turned out no; each one fought for himself." He then acknowledged that there were variations in the components of nationalism, and moreover, he said, it was largely accepted that the civil war was based on political divisions rather than religious ones. She was not sure whether she understood what he was implying. She commented carelessly that the task now was to decide what to remember and what to forget. This vision into his past triggered a dramatic silence. After that he had kissed her on the cheeks and walked away.

"What is his problem?" she screamed at him in Arabic after he left her and walked across the street. Several passers-by turned and stared, bewildered by her Arabic outburst.

Chapter 16

FOR MONTHS EVERY morning, she was assailed by the temptation to tell Elias how she felt towards him, but in the evening she would think, I ought not to tell him anything and keep it for myself. She was hampered by her suffering, asking herself, When shall I be reborn? and thinking, I've ruined myself. Yet at the same time, she thought it wasn't right to despair because of the turbulence he was creating in her life.

It was a bright morning when Elias called her and asked to see her in a nearby hotel the same afternoon. Room 21, he said. They met in the room; she wore a trim blue trouser suit and a red sleeveless top; he wore a black suit.

He grinned when she showed up.

"I thought you wouldn't come; you didn't sound keen."

She wasn't greatly impressed by his choice of meeting place.

"No, I am just surprised that we have to meet in a hotel, that's all."

He winked at her. "Better this way," he said.

Then he asked her to lie down on her front on the bed. He took his belt and whipped her back fiercely; then he tore her clothes. She didn't move; she was in a trance, calm and relaxed; she didn't even feel the pain. In a skimming motion, she grabbed his hands from behind and kissed them.

He said, "Now I've you," and then penetrated her from behind. Hurling into the shadow, they became one entity.

He then told her to kneel on the rough bathroom floor and give him a blow-job while he closed her nose, asphyxiating her. After a while he ejaculated in her mouth. Her knees were blistered, but she was happy to be his sex slave. She was convinced that by satisfying his sadistic desire, she will become irreplaceable, but his answer baffled her again.

"Did I perform OK?" she asked.

"I don't actually care," he said abruptly.

She stood up, feeling very stiff. He was standing beside her, impeccable in his suit, casting a long shadow across the room. She looked around the room, feeling humiliated, spent.

"My clothes are torn. I need your jacket so I can get out."

"Of course," he snapped.

She approached him, smiling indulgently, and held his hand. "Elias, are you happy at least?"

There was something slightly odd about him. "Yes, I'm happy, and you?"

"I am a bit tired, you know...I feel hungry; could we go somewhere and eat?"

Elias reflected a minute. "I can't. I have too many things to do."

He sounded moody today, and she glanced at him very calmly.

"I thought we could discuss today."

"Why? Discuss what? Why do we always have to discuss things? Why can't you just let it go?"

She paid no attention to his mood, but she knew that the meeting was coming to an end.

"OK. Call me, as I need to give your jacket back," she said and walked away.

After that they rarely made love. Once she called him and insisted on meeting in his house, and he consented grudgingly but then changed his mind and chose the same hotel where again they had rough sex. He didn't whip her this time; he just went on for hours, not caring whether she reached climax or not.

He grabbed her hair from behind and penetrated her violently, sometimes blocking her nose, bringing her to asphyxiation. It was not love; it was revenge— a sadistic feeling she had to surrender to. Otherwise he wouldn't enjoy it. She liked being his sexual slave and didn't care whether she enjoyed it or not or if it meant anything to him.

Afterwards she whispered in his ear, "When I first met you and spoke to you of what was bothering my soul, I felt transcendent and withdrawn from the world of war and hatred into heavenly places."

He smiled at her fertile imagination and her unequivocal innocence. He hugged her back tight in his arms, avoiding her eyes, and felt her breathing. He gave no reply and felt no qualms. He struggled to relate to any of her memories. Where did they come from? For him this nostalgia for a romantic past did not exist. He gazed at her but looked through her, his mind displaced. For one blink of an eye, his mind was still, and she must have caught this stillness and saw in it love—or was it? For once his silence was a comfort to her; her worries were resolved and she went home content. Elias regretted the way he made love to her; he wasn't proud of himself. He couldn't understand why he didn't make love to her the same way he did to Sally or Ella. The only explanation he could think of was perhaps deep down he wanted her to hate him as he didn't deserve her. He wanted to punish himself and for her to hate him and leave him. She is part of his past—a past that he wanted to forget and to erase forever.

A week later he called asking to see her in the same hotel. Then he said, "I have a big problem, and I'm trying to work it out. If I can't I'll definitely tell you about it—it's a struggle between image and reality." His words betrayed his self-awareness as an exile in the unbearable plight of someone who had witnessed a horrific act.

When she appeared at his door, she saw his blue eyes distractedly gazing around the room.

"Are you OK?" she asked.

She didn't want to venture any further. His small confession on the phone encompassed all their past history. It was more implicit than explicit, the beginning of what she saw as love and trust.

He said, "From my point of view, I am the only complete, albeit unwitting, witness to the truth."

He drank a glass of whiskey and then took her to bed. Wordlessly he avoided kissing her and took her violently from behind. Afterwards she felt overwhelmed. He ran to the toilet to wash himself while she lay on the bed full of his semen. He stood looming over her, like a winner after a long battle, like Achilles against Priam, looking at the crowd, proud, thanking the Gods. It wasn't a war, she thought, or was it? She asked to be his slave, not an equal opponent so why was he the winner? She had given him the title from the first moment they met; she had already awarded him the laurel wreath so why then was he so proud of his manhood, as if he'd won a victory over her? But, she thought, when the hero falls, he will be burned on the pyre.

"You think it is going to work?" she asked.

"What is going to work?" he said with a shrug.

"Us?"

"Us? Do you think there is an 'us'?"

She felt dragged into a corner, but she fought back proudly.

"Yes, I think so," she cried. "What do you call all this then? I am not your hooker-stripper."

She felt like smashing the mirror she saw reflecting her face. He peered at the sky through the window and said nothing. He seemed to have woken from his reverie and, looking at her, said sadly, "I don't know. It's complicated—complicated."

"What is complicated? I cannot get through to you. We are here alone thousands of kilometres away—why? I could make it work I promise you. I will give you everything you need; just stay with me," Laura cried.

It was evident that Elias did not want to elaborate but just wanted to end this conversation. All these feelings were not that important to him anymore; he was bothered by these long discourses. He didn't want to change; he was satisfied with his life and wanted no more attachments.

She was destroyed; she'd lost what she thought she had won. She leaned forward her face in her hands. Elias could not guess what was happening in her head. His ambiguous feelings and his refusal to talk about them assailed her. She looked around the room. "Damn it," she muttered. "Damn all my life!" The seconds piled up into an eternity, yet there was no noise, no movement, only his heavy breathing filling the dazzling white room.

Elias could feel his anger mounting. He lay back in his chair and looked at the view outside. "Holy shit," he murmured. Laura stared at him; there was a glow in his face, and then the light dimmed, and he felt a great dull weight on his chest, and darkness surrounded him.

He sat up. "Control yourself," he shouted. "What is the matter with you? We haven't seen each other for over ten years, and here you are wanting to control my life, my feelings, as if you know me."

"Yes, you're right. I thought I knew you; actually I don't, and you have become a monster," she said.

"Here we go with your discourse of guilt—just like my mother."

"Well, maybe she has a point after all; you lost your soul."

"My soul? What do you know about me and my soul? Why do you despise me? How dare you judge me? I opened my heart and my life to you, and you are sitting here judging me."

"I am not judging you. I am just trying to understand why you hate me so much."

"I don't hate you. I have done my best to shield myself from these criticisms. I left Lebanon for that. Please can you leave now? I have lots of work. I'll call you."

He didn't share his thoughts; he kept everything to himself and close to his heart. It was impossible to get through to him or to understand him, let alone to communicate with him. He showed her his blog, but it gave her little more insight to his true soul. The contents were dynamic and wide ranging. He wrote about love and the potential for love. Love as an arrow coming back or a sharp pain in the head. Loving a girl or a country; lovers kissing or posing in photographs and pretending to kiss. Once he wrote that in front of direct questions and issues, his answer would be oblique and never straight. Truth, he added, is not always good to hear, and it's usually better to hide it.

He wrote that we sent humans to the moon and explored the universe, but we failed to understand the people around us by simply walking into townships and *favelas* and talking to the inhabitants. We have paid billions of dollars to put satellites in orbit around the earth but do not make an effort to stop in the street and speak with a poor man or an abandoned child and ask how they ended up this way. We are powerful and mighty in wars and genocides but so frail and weak in front of small bacteria and viruses that destroy us. We always gave lectures and lessons about how to behave, wrote books about exemplary ways of life, learned how to say thank you, and were upset when we didn't receive thanks in return but were never bothered when someone decided to close their door and stay alone with their misery. We are more concerned about manners than about feelings. We should dedicate at least one day a year or take one dollar or one peso and give it to the poor. Maybe then, he wrote, we would make a better world instead of being barricaded in our houses behind bars in isolation and loneliness. What a hypocritical world it is, he said, where political ideas should be defended for the sake of power. We should expand our horizons beyond religious and nationalistic identities. Imperialist claims had yielded horrifying results; correcting these errors would be one of the most demanding tasks that could challenge us over the coming decades. He suggested that a fundamental problem facing humanity was that we really did not have a universal theory of a perfect life. Instead we are desperately trying to find another life with the assumption that we can find a new planet in the universe and so escape the mess we have created. We struggle to deal with death, but even stars die. What is it about our obsession with the past, the strangeness of the past, the pernicious uses of the past?

Why did he use the word "past" so many times? She asked him, but he answered furiously.

"Why are you spying on my thoughts; they don't belong to you."

"What do you mean? We have shared thoughts; we fought the same war, and we had the same enemy."

"No, you're wrong. We never fought the same war; it was incumbent upon me to ensure the safety of my neighbourhood." By equating war with safety, he knew he was venturing onto fragile territory.

"Why do you care anyway? It was a long time ago. You're always looking for a reason to fight me, to diminish me; why do you hate me so much?"

"I don't hate you. I don't love you. I don't feel anything towards anybody."

"Why?"

Laura was distraught; nothing could have hurt her more than his words.

"You never want to make love to me, and yet why did you just make love to me?" she demanded.

"Stop asking me all these questions. I made love to you because you asked me to."

"What happened to you, Elias? What happened in 1982?"

"Why are you asking me this, Laura? I mean why this particular date?"

"No particular reason…I just never saw you after that. That's all."

They went on talking openly, more freely. He told her that he had no choice but to leave. Many of his friends were wounded in the fighting and some died.

"So why were you fired from the phalangists?" she asked.

"No; I decided to leave, but I had to lie in front of Mounir so I didn't look like a coward."

"But why?"

"I think if I had stayed for a few more days, then I would have lost my humanity."

Elias seemed to find it hard to keep up the conversation without contradicting himself. She felt he was trying to balance what was essentially an unbalanced story. Tactically he walked onto the balcony and lit a cigarette. She didn't know whether to leave or to stay. She sat nervously, quietly, feeling like an idiot. What was she doing here? She remembered Philippe and how he went on his knees begging her to stay, crying at a bus stop, but still she walked away telling herself not to look back. She cherished him now; she felt she should have stayed with him.

"Tell me." She nudged him, but he turned away awkwardly to avoid answering.

"Nothing. I just left after. I don't want to be reminded of this heroic past—it was a relic. We like to adorn the past and think that we come from a great nation or the most beautiful country. I don't think like this anymore."

Despite the tension she thought of the evening as a good one. "You are very self-aware. I'm just trying to get to know you again," she laughed. "I just want to get the chance to know you. Do you miss your mum?"

"A bit, but I don't think about it."

She got up and hugged him, tried to grab his penis with her hand, but he gently pushed her away.

"I want to make love or sex, as you call it."

"Not here. In the room, and the way I like it."

She nodded submissively and followed him.

A steady rain had been falling for days, and there was nowhere to go. It was a Sunday, and her daughter Leila had a play date, so she was hoping to alleviate her boredom by opening the gallery. She pulled a great red wool coat around her shoulders and sat near the window in darkness and then hit the switch; the light dangling from the ceiling flashed on to illuminate the bare concrete floor.

Just then the doorbell rang, and when she opened it, Elias was there. He looked around, a grin spreading over his sharply boned face.

"Come in! This is a nice surprise!" said Laura. She studied him as he stood by the door. "Why did you come? I mean how did you know I was here?"

"No, I didn't. I just saw the light, that's all, and as I was passing by…do you mind if I stay?"

"Oh no, of course not! Please come in. It's just that I can't figure it out; you seem to want to avoid me."

"What do you mean, Laura?"

"I don't know. I haven't seen you for ages; you haven't been returning my calls, and I sent you lots of messages."

"Yeah, you sent me hundreds of them. I was busy. I had to write this short essay about life and death for the local newspaper; do you remember?"

"No, you didn't mention it."

"Ah."

"So why you? Out of all the people in town."

"What do you mean? Obviously because I am Lebanese."

"So they assume you have something to say…anyway what were your views on that?"

"Nothing. I have nothing to say to these people."

"Don't tell them anything, Elias; just tell me."

"Well, the main issue I have with these things is how we define them first before talking about them—like 'what is life?' They call it that, and at the other end of the spectrum, they call it death, but which one is the true appellation? Is life really life and death really death? Or could life be called death and for some death is life?"

"Why do people see it as a kind of a circle—a closure? Why not a linear concept with a continuation of the essence but under a different form. If we explain the notion scientifically or rather rationally between a beginning and a termination, the 'in-between' could be called life or a stage, a passage, a gift or a sacrifice, if we look at it from the Christian point of view. 'Life is too short,' 'We only have one life,'—these expressions seem to be very popular now; everyone uses them, but are they actually the truth? Life is not short, not long—it is just what it is. Adding a value on numbers won't change any fact or behaviour; why should we know the span of it in order to live it or to fear not to live it? Some people achieve in short lives what others can't do in a long life-span. Some spend a whole life without leaving an impression; nobody hears their voices or traces their souls. Sometimes knowing its end could help us to reach the stars rather than spending a lifetime gazing at them. What does time do for us? It's irreversible; it binds us instead of liberating us, and it enslaves us and limits us. If life could be measured, then how could tangibility meet spirituality? The notion of past, future, and present is flawed. The present moment doesn't exist per se as what I said is already the past and what I am saying is already the future; then within that there is a distant past and a distant future. Kant said time vanishes and begins anew every instant. Where do we live? What is the now? Some of us live in the past as if we had the luxury of wasting time. It's difficult not to as we all are the fruit of the past. What we lose we cannot regain. We are all so busy chasing shadows, demons, and fears that we forget what we are experiencing and what is waiting for us."

"There is a path, whether you believe in destiny or in free will," Laura interrupted his discourse. "Another dilemma that goes inside the dilemma itself of life or death." She believed in destiny, and within it there was a limited free will that some would call "timing." "Timing is a quintessential element of life that rules everything, every moment of it."

He went on with his monologue, ignoring what she had just said. "Life is encoded with laws and morality, but it is here because nobody minds these laws; they are there to remind us about how to live a 'good life.' It is a code that could be religious or not. How to live should be taught, and it seems that if nobody follows the book of life, then chaos reigns. We are so used to this code that not following it is like dancing on one leg, and we risk failing in human justice. Again this has its flaws; some people are afraid of God's reaction on the other side, or they believe in karma as an earthly punishment. What is right now was wrong before. Women being thrown on funeral pyres in India when they became widows is now seen as an aberration, but originally it was seen as the right thing to do, so what is right in the book of life, and what is wrong?"

He didn't believe in any morality or any code and mocked people who did. "Life should not have any limitation; it is as vast as this earth and what lies beyond it," he once said.

"The building blocks of life can be found throughout space. I can travel with my soul virtually everywhere, so why should my body have limitations?"

"Your soul is a bird, and your body is a cage," she answered.

"Well, then you should liberate your soul. St. Augustine said that the mind should be that of an individual soul but by no means that of a 'world soul.' For Aristotle time is not a movement, and it requires a soul to distinguish instants and count intervals." Elias answered.

"How should I let my soul exist?" Laura asked.

"You are everything I couldn't achieve; don't stop here. Listen to music; go somewhere beyond any possibility. I've tried everything. I went to the limit of my existence and feelings. I actually loved and lived even if it didn't work. I just tested my madness until I collapsed. I went to the end and then came back unsatisfied; you know why? Because I didn't commit. Commitment is huge. It's an investment, and I don't think I have it in me. I am a nomad. There is no point in you getting attached to me. I won't anchor you anywhere. No port is waiting for me, no city either—just the void. I pushed myself so far that it is too late to come back to myself. I went too far. Why me, Laura? I am not good for you or your daughter. Go fly; don't wait for me. I'm empty. I was dead the moment I left Lebanon. I left my heart there. I tried to find happiness in other women's arms, but I failed, and I brought misery to them. In the name of conquest, I walked on my uncle's heart Just to get Sally, and yet when she was mine, I didn't want her. Like the Brazilian stripper, I became the pole she needed to dance on; she needed me to exist, but for me it was too late the moment she went for the pole. But at the time, it was a matter of life and death. Sally helped me financially after my uncle was killed. Nobody knew what I was going through. I was alive for appearances' sake, but I was dead inside. I dread looking at the past. It's hideous, and with it all my dreams and expectations are gone."

"What about the future, Elias?"

"What future? How can someone like me dream about a future? I am an artist, and I can barely make ends meet. I live in a small room. I use it as a studio and a home. I sell my paintings to the rich and mighty, and they don't see me as an artist—only as a means to their own wealth. They hang my paintings in their penthouses and show them to their friends as the latest investment, but they never ask me about how I felt when painting it. They cast a shadow on me."

"Don't worry; I don't want your money or your paintings. I just want your soul."

"That's even worse, Laura."

By now it was late afternoon. She was still struggling to understand him.

"Hang on a minute," she said and then gestured that she needed to go upstairs where it was quieter. After a monumental effort, she reached the stairs, opened the window, and felt the sultry air; her eardrums felt like they were about to burst. "Sorry about that," she said.

He ran his fingers through her shoulder-length hair.

"Don't worry; I am just telling you that you are much better without me."

"Could you stop!" she shouted. "For once in your life, could you stop and listen to what I have to say? This matter doesn't only concern you; it is our story, and you can't just close the page and go. This is a lifetime. I've known you since I was a child. I can't just let you go with all the pride I have. I just can't let you go. I had my share also. You never asked me what happened when I left Lebanon; you never asked me about my ex-husband or my daughter. You don't want even to see her, so stop with your pathetic discourse about my well-being and happiness. Be true to yourself and to me for once. You owe it to me to tell the truth. Why should we always make love in a hotel or—sorry as you call it 'have sex'—why? Why not in your bed? I don't understand."

She began to pace up and down the room in her agitation.

"It's a bloody mystery. Are we together or not? Who am I to you? Sally saved you from your financial problem and the Brazilian from your solitude. What is my role? What am I saving you from?"

After a long silence, she said, "Oh, I see; maybe I'm not? Maybe I am adding to your problems—just say it once and for all. Screw you!" she added jokingly, trying to break the tension.

His face darkened. After a pause he said, "Aren't you being a bit melodramatic? These things can happen—that two people can't find happiness in the presence of each other. Why be so pessimistic about our lives?"

Laura's buried sadness found a voice. "You know you've been acting very weirdly since the first day I saw you. You're right. I'm not making you happy, nor are you making me happy, but maybe if I knew a bit more of your life and you knew a bit more of my life, then maybe it could work. We always look for changes from the outside instead of sometimes doing our best to work with what we have."

She wrapped her hands around his shoulders and gave him a motherly hug. He stood there like an ice cube, keeping his arms folded. A sickening feeling of loneliness swelled inside of her, and she said, "Please say something; please, I beg you."

"Laura, you don't want to listen. You are asking me to speak, but you are dreading what I am about to say."

Fearing what would come next, she knew deep in her heart that if she pushed him too much, he would reveal terrible things. Something did not feel right, and her imaginings flooded back. She saw something sinister and tragic in his eyes.

"I am a bit on edge; that's all. I have to close the gallery. Diego won't like it. But before that just answer this question—what makes you alive?"

"What do you mean by alive? I am alive."

She took her keys from her cheap bag. He turned the light off, and they headed outside, but her hands were shaking so much that the keys slipped from her grasp and fell into the gutter, narrowly missing the drain. He picked them up and handed them to her.

"Are you OK? Your hands are shaking. That was lucky."

"What do we do next? Do you have any plans?" she asked.

"No," he replied and then blocked her path.

"Look, listen to me; I like you a lot, but things are not that easy." His face was bright red, and his eyes were burning.

"You have someone in your life. I am sure you are hiding it from me—someone taller and much prettier than me."

"Why do you need to compare yourself with people? Everyone is unique."

"Really? Do you find me pretty?"

"Why is it that important that I find you pretty? What does this change in our relationship?"

She covered her eyes and started crying. They slowly stepped out from the crowded pavement. "Make love to me tonight please."

"And your daughter?"

"I will call my friend and ask her if she can stay with her a bit longer. Do we really have to book a hotel?"

"Yes, it would be better." She was taken aback by his severe tone.

"Are you angry with me?"

"No." He returned her anxious glance. "Just worried."

"About what?"

"About you not understanding me."

They walked to the usual local hotel. The bed was immaculately made; she headed for the bathroom flinging the door open, and a faint hint of his aftershave hung in the air. From the bathroom mirror, she saw him sitting on the edge of the bed.

"You know I have a problem in dealing with reality. The trauma that the war left on both of us is an existentialist one, not just historical. We ended up moving to different stages. When the war took our people, we were shattered with pain, but when it took our enemy, it was an occasion for *jouissance*. There was a dearth of prolonged mourning rituals after each death; we had no time, and we had to move on quickly maybe to avoid coming to terms with death and injustice. Mourning requires names, but we didn't have them. I only learned about the sacredness of a human being since I left Lebanon. We never had the choice of reliving the past and re-enacting it in order to heal rather than blaming others. But the past is the past, and it is made that way so we don't disturb it. What is the point of coming to terms with it if it doesn't exist anymore? It is only a recollection of memories, and memories, and a narrative. Finding a harmony with this narrative instead of avoiding it is important—a way to self-heal. Shifting from the past in order to idealize it is a big mistake."

"It depends," said Laura. "How do you look at the past, Elias? From an idealized view or not, is history an arena? I was only a spectator during the war, and maybe this is why I would like to keep myself that way."

"How can you separate yourself from that arena?" Elias asked. "You had to define boundaries with a valid status, differentiating roles from one another—one is a killer, and one is the victim. But it doesn't work like that. Sometimes the victim was the killer. You can't just forget the past and take a leap into the future—that's a very romantic approach."

"Then what do you want me to do?" Laura demanded. "Just sit and think about it every day forgetting I have a life to live? What will the past bring me? Everything that the past brought me until now was misery, and I have to fight now to get this misery off me so I can live."

"The danger of your thinking is that evil comes from an external elite who decided on our behalf that actually evil is in us and that we are all guilty," Elias interjected.

"Sometimes understanding is madness. Believe me; you need to move forward," she answered.

"I saw more dead than you, Laura."

"So how did you feel?"

"I felt nothing, I felt dead myself. I identified myself with them, a sort of carnivalesque scene where all of us were part of the same weakness and disempowerment or abjection of the human being."

"How can you see a fantasy in trauma?"

"Because we are all victims. You are turning the problem into one of memory, saying that we should try to forget the past, and I am talking about living it even on the periphery of consciousness.'

"You seem to have a desire to stay in an impasse and to bring others into it. It seems too simple to satisfy yourself with just one narrative that is geared towards victimization and to turn everything and everyone into accomplices."

He sat with his head resting in his hands, staring blankly into space. Laura noticed his silence, but she knew him well enough to know that her words troubled him.

She quietly sat next to him and said, "When I was ten, years ago, we were at the beach once, and there was this man standing with his feet in the water smoking a cigarette when someone approached me and told me that he had killed a guy."

"So what did you do?" he asked snapping out of his reverie.

"Nothing; I just stared at him as long as I could."

"You thought he did it?"

"I am sure he was guilty, but I just couldn't imagine this guy capable of carrying out such a hideous act. I really thought that probably he had to do it back then," she said reflectively.

A tense silence descended for few seconds. He was sweating. The image of women and children running in all directions suddenly became clearer. For the first time, he could see the colours of their garments and their naked feet covered with dust. Their scarves scattered on the ground—a reminder of a humanity stripped of compassion, devoid of pity. Laura felt something was wrong. She kneeled in front of him and took his hands and kissed them. He took his shirt off and took her in his arms. After they finished her heart was pounding. With a huge effort, she heaved herself out of bed and winced as her bare feet touched the cold wooden floor. As usual sex was very rough, but for some reason she did not enjoy it this time—not only because of the physical pain but because of the sudden stark reality that things were not going in the right direction. She crept quietly to the bathroom and eased the door shut. She sat in the toilet cubical and started crying.

She ran water into the basin to wash herself. The water was boiling, and she needed to forget herself in that hot water. Elias followed her to the bathroom and stared at her. She felt very ashamed of her naked body; she flinched and automatically covered her breasts.

"You have always made love this way?"

He seemed annoyed at her question. "For God's sake, you have been asking me questions since early evening. What is troubling you? You speak about forgetting the past, and the only thing you want to do is to dig up mine." He raised his hand and sharply slapped it down on the bathroom worktop.

She shivered. She knew she should have left him a long time ago, but he always allayed any niggling doubts by hugging her afterwards, his way of showing remorse or contrition in a way that Laura forgave him immediately.

"Sorry," he said confused.

Laura rubbed her wrist and sighed with relief.

"Your past is running rampant to the point of obsession, and I didn't mean to evoke the past in that sense," she said. "It's just that when the present can't heal the past, the vacuum is filled with trauma. I think perhaps you need to mourn more."

"That's a truncated view of the past. It's more complex than that, and by putting the past as a memory, you are dealing with boundaries, which I told you about earlier," Elias exclaimed. "For me this past has no boundaries. I don't know where to begin. The past should be based on empathy undisturbed by critical judgment. We just have to relive it."

"Sometimes I have the feeling you lived through something terrible, and you are hiding it from me."

Elias went on to fleetingly evoke cheerful moments from his past; the appeal to lost innocence shadowed his memory. His expression of guilt was disguised as a detached voice within himself; for him guilt was collective. He insistently turned away from sole responsibility, as that would expose him to different and perhaps dangerous realities. He knew his own limitations and the manner in which he was prone to act. Deep inside he knew that Laura would be the only one who could heal him; he did not need to relive his past. In fact his discourse on the past was little more than a dumb excuse to hold back and hide from his fear to love her.

Laura finished bathing and then slowly dressed herself. Then she kissed him on his lips, and he pulled her into his arms. "Yes, I always made love this way," he muttered. She was not sure how to respond and glared at him in disbelief. Then she leaned against him, welcoming the comfort of his hands. "You are a good man," she said. He looked away slightly embarrassed.

"I won't keep you any longer," he said. "You must go back to your daughter."

Chapter 17

DAYS PASSED BY, and Laura's malaise and frustration grew steadily. She always had to call and text Elias as he never attempted to contact her. She had a terrible migraine, so she swallowed an aspirin and went downstairs and out into the fresh air. She stumbled slightly and grabbed the handrail; then she sat down on the glossy red steps outside the gallery facing the sun. The thrill of anticipation reclaimed her thoughts; maybe she would see him walking past. She had sat waiting there an hour when he came walking slowly towards her, rested his elbows on the rail with a casual confidence, and gave her a quick kiss.

He looked at her with concern. "Are you feeling sick? You look pale."

"I didn't sleep well."

"Maybe you should take something."

"Yeah, maybe. What did you do last night?"

"Last night? Oh the usual—stayed in the apartment."

"Why didn't you call?"

"I don't know. I thought maybe you were busy with your daughter."

"She has someone looking after her, you know."

She had never questioned that trust before now, but something in the way he squirmed slightly under her gaze made her doubtful.

"Even if I am at home, you can always come over and have a drink."

"I am not a social type; you know that. I like to keep to myself."

"Yes, but we are two foreigners in this village, and we have known each other for so long; it seems weird that both of us should stay alone in our homes."

Reluctantly he drew closer to her and put his finger on her lips. "It's OK, Laura; why are you so stressed and always on the offensive? Please cool down."

She offered a slight shrug in response and then let out a frustrated sigh. "I'm sorry."

"Where did you think I was?" his eyes narrowed.

"Nowhere. I mean I don't know. Should I doubt you?" she looked at him.

"No, I'm just asking."

"I always feel under inquisition with you."

She couldn't keep the agitation from her voice. She breathed out through her nose and forced herself to calm down; she was terrified of losing him. She felt so guilty.

"I'm sorry. Look, really I'm sorry. I'm on edge; that's all."

"Don't apologize. People are a burden, and you shouldn't burden yourself. We all start out lovers and end up feeling the weight of the presence of the other. The moment I felt it, I always stopped loving," Elias said in a soothing voice.

"You speak as if love is a rational feeling that we decide to start and stop."

"Probably not, but for me it always seemed to be the case."

"Come in; I will make you a cup of tea."

"No, I have to go, Laura. I will be in touch soon."

After weeks of silence, Elias finally returned Laura's calls, using work as an excuse for not answering her sooner.

"Hey, how are you, Laura?"

She sounded distraught. "I can't take it anymore, Elias," she shouted. "You've been treating me worse than a maid—with no respect or consideration. Do you know I left the world and my husband just to be here with you?"

"What do you mean your husband? You told me you came here by pure coincidence."

"No, I didn't. Mary called your mother, and that's how I knew you were here."

"So you followed me? But for what? There was no promise or a word from me; how can you build a life on a mirage?"

"I thought we could work it out. I thought you loved me."

"Laura." There was a silence. "How can you put yourself in such a situation?"

"Why did you never return my calls?"

"Because I was busy. I genuinely have to pay my rent every month. I have to work hard for this."

"You never cared about me; you only care about yourself."

"OK, Laura, could you calm down please? I don't recognize you. I think you're not well."

"No, I'm all right; it's just that you make me feel like shit."

"Why do you say that? Look, I'm sorry."

"I did everything you wanted. What a fool I was. I mean you never met my daughter, and I have never been to your studio. I know nothing about your past."

"Laura, I told you that I am a lost cause. There is nothing glorious about my past—nothing worth knowing about. I did bad things in my past that I am ashamed of, and I don't deserve you."

"Like what? Try to talk to me. Just tell me something. I love you, and I don't mind even if you have committed a murder."

"You don't know my past."

"No, I don't. That's the sad reality."

"Don't be sad. I don't want to upset you. You're a very good person. Look, I want to take you somewhere nice so we can spend the weekend together; what do you think?"

"You mentioned it in the past, but then you never honour your promises," she said harshly; the words seemed abrupt and cold as she rushed to get them out.

"I know, but now let's do it. Look, take the train and then from there you take a taxi, and it's an hour and a half journey, but it's a very beautiful landscape. Later on I'll drop you the brochure with the map through your letterbox. Does that sound good?"

"When should I go?" she asked calmly.

"Next weekend? You could go on Saturday, and then I'll follow you."

"We come back on Sunday?"

"Yes, on the Sunday, late morning."

"Why late morning?"

"Because I have this rich woman coming to my studio to paint her. She said around three p.m.; would that be OK? Then you can't leave your daughter any longer, can you?"

"True, but why don't we go together, Elias?"

"Because I have an urgent matter to settle, but I will come around five p.m. Don't worry; you won't even feel the time. You'll be in the swimming pool looking at the mountains sipping your tequila."

"OK."

Chapter 18

SHE SAT SILENTLY on the edge of the bed, thinking about the events of September 16, 1982, the Sabra and Shatila massacre. Four days later was the last time she saw Elias until their meeting in Brazil. How could she have forgotten about it? It was part of her childhood. It was not the only event she could not recall; she wondered though if it was now a collective memory. She recalled reading that Foucault had argued that popular memory was a form of collective knowledge possessed by people who were barred from writing, from producing their books themselves, and from drawing up their own historical accounts. People nevertheless do have a way of recording history, of remembering it, or of keeping it fresh, and using it. Laura thought that we could share a sort of memory but not the same experience. The only memory of hers was that her brother's birthday was on September 14 and that day her father was shaving in the bathroom when a huge explosion was heard and felt across Beirut. She ran and switched on the radio to hear that the newly elected president, Bechir Gemayel, had escaped an assassination attempt, but in reality, it became clear later he had died instantly. They had to lie in order to calm the young phalangists who would immediately seek revenge. When the news of his death finally broke, the doom of revenge was sealed. Suddenly the street became a desert; only cats and dogs wandered around. She was devastated. She could recall the sadness she could feel when hope was taken away, and there was no future. Elias was one of the youths affected by this madness. He had been expelled from the phalangists for bad behaviour, but he didn't explain the reason. She remembered seeing him agitated on the night of September 18. Thinking about it now, she wondered, Was he part of a bigger thing? A group of neighbours and friends were sitting on the wall of her building sharing a beer. Normally they were a noisy crowd, but not that night; they were murmuring—the silence around them made the darkness of that night heavier than usual.

Looking at them from the corner of the living room window, pulling the old thick curtain, her father interrupted her nervously asking what she was doing in the dark. She replied, "Nothing; just having a feel of the night." Her father said in his usual undermining tone, "How can you feel the night? It is only dusk." She answered impatiently, "Look I'm a bit bored and have nothing to do." She was careful as any words could have triggered his violent character.

It was not appropriate for a girl to go and chat with boys, unless she had an excuse, and it was very difficult for her not to participate in their conversation. Her mother saved her. Few minutes later she asked her if she would take the rubbish bag downstairs. She agreed instantly, which surprised her mum. She put on her high heels and some eyeliner, snatched the bag, and went very quickly down the stairs directly to the big black bin when the three boys greeted her. She looked into Elias's eyes, and in that late afternoon, she could smell the weed; he gazed at her in silence. Mounir grabbed her hands and asked her to stay.

"All OK?" she asked.

"Yeah; Elias is a bit sick." Mounir answered her looking at Elias.

"Why? What happened? Has he eaten something wrong? Anyway we are all sick after what happened…the assassination."

"We all start as king and queen of hearts; then life transforms us to queens and kings of spades," Elias replied in a violent tone.

"I am sorry. I didn't mean to…why are you shouting at me?" she answered tearfully.

Mounir intervened, trying to calm Elias. "Hey, hey. Calm down, OK."

"I am calm." Then he turned towards Laura. "By the way what are you sick about again?"

"Oh my God, I am only expressing my opinion. We should stop this rampant impunity in our country. Everybody should account for their behaviour…"

"We're all waiting for you, Mrs. Justice! Come on, do your investigation. Who killed Bechir? You seem to know everything about this world. Standing here giving us lessons about morality and justice."

"Is that why your shirt is stained with blood? Is this justice for you?"

"What do you mean?" Elias answered her with a jumpy tone.

"I didn't mean anything...it was a joke, and by the way it is a figure of speech...you look jumpy tonight. I'd better go back home."

Laura walked back home. She was in a terrible mood. "Of course he doesn't like me; it's so obvious," she thought.

Now she recalled this. She wished she could have asked him what happened that night. Christian phalangists took their revenge. They headed to the two Palestinian camps and slaughtered many people. At least between seventeen hundred and two thousand women and children were murdered in a savage extermination; it was like releasing wolves among sheep. We Christians were supposed to be the sheep, she thought. This time the roles were reversed; the victim becomes the assassin. A stigma on our history—revenge always calls for new blood. Spectacles of death, the scattering of the bodies and their disposal reflected their social marginality. She thought that unlike the ancient world where gladiatorial combat made death a sport, here there was an abhorrence of violence exposed publicly, but in fact the actuality of violence did not change. We live in a society where animal hunting was considered distasteful but not the butchering of human beings. The mounds of cadavers of women and children as human scapegoats and shields demonstrated not just a failed society but also a failed humanity. War ceased to be a fair game but a disillusionment of civilization.

On the nineteenth in the morning, the news of the massacre was broadcast everywhere. On every lip there was fear of retaliation. While going to the local deli to buy some rice and bread, she saw Elias walking towards her building. She tried to catch his eyes, but he was completely withdrawn and cold. His eyes looked lost as if there was no life in him. She turned around and pretended she had left her money behind at home, so she followed him. At the stairs of the building, Elias told her he was going to see his friend Mounir.

"Sorry about the way I spoke to you yesterday...I was drunk."

"I forgive you. I was provocative too, Elias."

She hesitated and wanted to hug him, to kiss him, to tell him how much she loved him. How much she would stop everything to be with him, to run away with him. She hated her despot father who frowned upon every boy around her; she knew that Elias was a very good man and that he would look after her. He was nineteen and she was seventeen. She did not care about her studies or the convent school and all the bitches in her class. They always looked down at her as she was the poorest among them. Here there was no competition, and she wanted Elias above everything. But Elias did not have the same feelings towards her. He was definitely older than nineteen after that day and could have been one hundred years old. His heart just shut down—no beating, no pumping, just stationery as a piece of art. No feelings or regret—he had buried Elias forever.

Now when she looked in his eyes, she still saw the remains of sadness, profound and pure like his blue eyes. The same gaze she saw in September 1982. The reconstructions of the days that followed weaved together in her mind, and Elias was part of it. Free will and complicity played a major role in his decision.

The events of September 16 had definitely shaped his life forever. He did not only kill children and women, he also sacrificed his innocence, his teenage years, his childhood, and the rest of his life. The discovery of this reality persuaded her that she had discovered a new image of Elias's reality. Memory preserved our awareness of our inner life; it brought the past to the present. In forgetting the past, the present then seemed irrelevant, empty, and senseless.

-->==() (==<-

On Saturday morning, on August 9, 1997, just before Laura took the train as promised to meet Elias at Sally's hotel, Elias went to see a lawyer to deal with his will as Giuseppe had left him a decent amount of money. Before he did so, he called Sally.

"Hello, Elias, what can I do for you?"

"Hello, Sally, I just want to book a room for one person into your hotel."

"Oh, now you don't want to come to my house; you prefer my hotel?"

He laughed. "No, it's just for a friend. She'll be checking in today in the late afternoon."

"She...? She's a friend or a girlfriend? And who is she anyway?"

"Well, she's a childhood friend from Lebanon."

"I see. OK. I'll give her the best room I have."

"Do you mean the one that has the view of your horses?"

"Exactly; there's a beautiful view, and it's the sunniest and most peaceful room I have."

"Thank you, Sally."

"Will you be joining her?"

"No, not really. Ah, I will send a parcel to her; please send it to her room when you get it," he replied.

She sighed. "No problem. So I won't see you then."

"You will, but not this weekend," he said decisively.

After the phone call, he walked across the street to the lawyer. It was a dusty old office with a dirty carpet, and behind the desk stood a young lawyer in his thirties. He wore dark glasses with a white shirt and a plain blue tie.

"Hi, it's Elias, I guess?"

"Yes, we spoke on the phone."

"Absolutely. What can I do for you Elias?"

"Well, I inherited some money from my uncle, and I wanted to make a will with this money, in case something happens to me."

"You're still very young, but you're right. Life is unpredictable; it's a wise decision," the lawyer said.

"Great."

"I'll ask my secretary to come over so she can take notes of your wishes."

"Of course."

An old lady appeared through the door. "Hello, sir," she said and sat down and looked at Elias. "I'm listening."

Elias hesitated a bit and then leaned back on his chair. "I'd like to give everything...I, Elias Badawi, want to leave Laura Malak and her daughter all I possess from my current paintings to my bank account in case I die. I want her to bury my ashes in the local cemetery and leave a portion of the ashes to give to my mother."

"OK, but please can you spell her family name for me."

"Of course; M-a-l-a-k."

"Thank you. I'll type this up; then you can sign it. Please give me your passport."

The secretary left the room and a fizz of nerves surged up inside Elias. He felt dizzy; then with an embarrassed expression, he looked at the lawyer. "She is my childhood friend. We are both Lebanese. I want her to get everything I have," he said.

"Of course, no problem. Please write down her address and her phone number in case something happens, and we can notify her."

Elias wrote everything down, and once the secretary came with the typed letter, he signed it, kept a copy, and left.

-->==◉ ◉==<-

That afternoon Elias switched off his phone and went to his studio and tried to sleep. As usual his past came back to haunt him, but this time he was too tired to put these ugly memories behind him. Maybe they were coming back because he was not dealing with them; it was like an endless rally in a tennis match. Recently he'd tried to forget his past with several one-night stands; he didn't want any attachments. He wanted to break up his own focus by being decadent and hence triumphant, but for some reason today was different.

The cries of the children begging him not to slaughter them remained unchanged; the women wailing, running in the streets became louder and louder. Blood spattered all over the camps, leaving old men clawed to their mattresses with open guts. He not only watched it, he participated. He thought Laura could salvage him, but she had failed, and he was already in a sea of blackness. Most of his paintings were witnesses; he drew houses as cemeteries housing the dead living.

He tried to tell Laura, but words would not come out and got stuck in his dry throat; ashamed of the echo, they died on his lips. She had tried to understand him, but he couldn't tell her, because he knew that even she as a good person would turn her back on him and leave; who wouldn't? She was a mother after all and a constant reminder to him of Lebanon and their lost childhood.

He thought that he had loved Laura from the first moment he saw her, but then other things became a priority. He needed to assert himself; he was a warrior, a defender of faith, a revenger of a lost dream of reconciliation stolen by a wicked explosion in Achrafieh that day of the celebration of the cross.

All he knew then was revenge, and at that time it seemed the right thing to do. Wash away dishonour with dishonour; show them what it was to lose someone you loved.

The next morning he woke up and turned his phone on. There were many messages and a missed call from Laura and Sally. He didn't want to hear them. He dressed and headed to the train station and asked for a ticket for Las Montes. Once on the train, he texted Laura.

"Hey, it's me; don't be mad. I'm on my way; have to switch off phones as battery is dead...love you, Elias."

Once Laura said to him, "Do you know what the secret of love is?"

"No," he'd replied.

"Never be afraid to love more."

When he got off the train, he waved for a taxi and then changed his mind at the last minute when he saw a car-hiring agency. He filled out the paperwork, gave a photocopy of his driving license, and drove towards Last Montes. He didn't feel too confident as in Lebanon all driving licenses were forgeries, but the road was almost empty with barely any traffic. He decided to tell Laura the whole truth—no more lies or games. He wanted to have an honest relationship, but at the same time, would she forgive him? And what if she left him like Ella? He couldn't imagine his world without her. Would she think of him as a petty criminal hiding behind his paintings?

->==() ()==<-

Laura finished her breakfast. Her mood was very low; she toured the hotel and then saw two paintings by Elias hanging on the main stairs leading to Sally's personal apartment.

"Hi," said Audrey.

Laura turned her head. "Oh, hi."

"So how is your stay so far?"

"It's OK," replied Laura thoughtfully.

Then she pointed at the paintings. "I think I know the artist," she muttered. "Weird that they are displayed here."

"Why?" asked Audrey.

"I don't know. He's just not that well known, so I wonder how his paintings landed here."

"Oh, he's a good friend of Mrs. Gibbs."

"A good friend?" Laura asked.

"Yes. I don't know all the details, but I think she was a good friend of his uncle. By the way this package has just arrived for you along with this letter."

"I see; now I understand…oh, OK, thank you." Laura did not like the pitiful look Audrey gave her. Laura proudly said, "I've known him all my life; he's my childhood friend."

She went to her room and opened the package carefully. She found Elias's diary.

Laura's phone beeped; she took it from her pocket and saw Elias's text message. "On my way."

Laura did not want to text him back. She decided to restore a little of her pride. She went towards the pool with the diaries and sat under the sun looking at the magpies cooling themselves near the water's edge. She almost forgot herself. She asked the waiter for lemon juice while rehearsing in her head the scenario of her meeting with Elias. She determined not to be as distraught and petulant as she had been on the phone the day before, but she would demand answers to the many questions racing through her head. Where to start from, she thought. From Sally, or the Brazilian stripper, the studio, the paintings, or her daughter?

She first opened the letter.

"My love Laura,

It took me time, and it wasn't easy to write to you. I hope one day you can forgive me. I know you will because you stayed the same girl

I met in Lebanon. You haven't changed; lucky you. Life didn't corrode you; on the contrary in a way it has preserved you. Unlike me. Life threw me and then took me back. Moulded me and then left me loose, sent me to the end and then brought me back to the beginning. I am sorry about those women whom I have raped, those new born babies that I have thrown at the wall, and those men I have killed. I wanted so much to meet the survivors and to ask for forgiveness. I am not going give you excuses, nationalism, revenge for Bachir, alcohol and drugs supplied that day…no, Laura. I wasn't proud or happy or under drugs. I was ashamed. I walked on the streets with my machete looking at the dirt. I killed but never looked at their eyes. I slaughtered but never heard their cries. You know God controls everything except for one thing—love. He gave us the choice to follow the path of love or to leave it. That day I decided to leave it. Many things were spinning in my head—my mother's constant disappointment, my father's eyes, my burnt childhood, my rifle waiting to kill, my comrades shouting with joy…

Please forgive me because your forgiveness matters. I love you, and I need to be able to look you in the eyes one day—to be a good father for your daughter and a good husband for you. I want to believe that it is possible to do so that the sun is still shining and we could run on the beach as we did when we were kids."

Laura dropped the letter on the floor. She was in a total shock. She repeated the same words in a trance, like a mantra. "I love you, Laura." As she picked up the letter, the waiter came back. "Madam, you have a phone call at reception."

She smiled, thinking, Oh, now he's running after me, asking my forgiveness, so I'll try to play hard to get. She thought, I should have treated him this way a long time ago.

She headed towards the reception where Sally was standing, looking shocked and tearful. She looked at her and the distance to the phone seemed a lifetime; she knew deep inside exactly the news awaiting her. Laura sat trembling as Sally handed her the phone, and she took it calmly.

"Hello."

"Is this Laura Malak?"

"Yes."

"This is Chief Inspector Marcelo Katz."

"What can I do for you?"

"I am sorry I have to break such distressing news, but we have here the body of a young man who was killed in a car crash. We need you to come so you can identify the body."

Printed by Amazon Italia Logistica S.r.l.
Torrazza Piemonte (TO), Italy